I0548927

MADNESS ENDS

BETH D. CARTER

Madness Ends
ISBN # 978-1-78430-883-4
©Copyright Beth D. Carter 2015
Cover Art by Posh Gosh ©Copyright November 2015
Interior text design by Claire Siemaszkiewicz
Totally Bound Publishing

Published in 2015 by Totally Bound Publishing, Newland House, The Point, Weaver Road, Lincoln, LN6 3QN, United Kingdom.

Totally Bound Publishing is a subsidiary of Totally Entwined Group Limited.

MADNESS ENDS

Dedication

As always, thanks so much to my editor, Faith Bicknell-Brown. She pushed me to become a better writer and I'll be eternally grateful.

To my friends and beta readers: C.R. Moss, Jonella, Kate, Shannon, Allyson and Diane. Thank you so much for your time!

Chapter One

Kaiya Hanazawa, her gaze downcast, shuffled in silence behind her grandfather and two of his men into the small hospital. Her grandfather expected demureness from her, especially since she'd been returned after being kidnapped. The word bounced around in her mind like a ricocheting bullet. A shiver ran through her. She'd been very close to being sold into a human trafficking ring when she'd been snatched off the streets while attending a poetry symposium for the deaf. Had it not been for three brave bikers, there was no telling where she'd be. After her stint in a hospital, she'd been sent home and summarily carted back to the ancestral Hanazawa fortress. Forty-eight hours ago, she'd been in Japan, locked up behind walls and told she was there for her protection. Truthfully, she'd been there because her grandfather felt like a failure. He hadn't been able to protect her parents, and even with all the clout he wielded in Los Angeles, she had still been taken.

Her cousin, Chloe, had come to Bair, Nebraska, to find the man responsible for saving her and to thank him. Now she lay in a hospital bed, shot, and Kaiya didn't know what to think. Chloe had gone out of her way to free her from her grandfather's prison and yet, if she died…

Kaiya shook her head. She didn't want to think about that outcome, because if Chloe didn't make it, Kaiya would be forced back behind the safeguards of her family's ancestral home. Guilt slammed into her heart, making it ache. Her cousin fought for her life, and all Kaiya cared about was being a prisoner once more.

Her grandfather stopped at the waiting room and pointed.

"Wait," he ordered in Japanese.

She bowed and did as he commanded, even though she didn't want to. What she longed to do was scream at him. Hit him. Give him the finger and tell him to go fuck himself. But she didn't do any of those things. She never did. Her grandfather was one of the men she feared the most, and fear did many strange things to people.

Kaiya sat in the waiting room. She looked at everything, not missing one single detail. The seats were as comfortable as they could possibly be in a hospital, even though some of them had threadbare cushions. Dirt lined the baseboards, suggesting the cleaning crew didn't care all that much for cleanliness. The magazines were three months outdated. Kaiya only hoped the staff wasn't as lackadaisical as the administration seemed.

In the waiting room doorway, two big, muscular men appeared. She shifted her focus. Interest gripped her as the rich smell of leather tickled her nostrils. She inhaled deeply. Both men were tall, filling the doorway with enough brawn to send butterflies dancing through her belly. The name Men of Hell blazed across the backs of their leather jackets, letting her know these men were bikers. A devil face, nestled in flames, sat between the rockers with the club name on top and Bair, Nebraska on the bottom rocker. She'd read plenty of erotic romance to give her all sorts of delicious fantasies, especially from the man with his back toward her. He sported long, dark hair pulled into a small ponytail that would probably cover his shoulders when free. She slipped her gaze lower to a nice ass encased in black denim. She had an urge to bite those firm cheeks. Scuffed black riding boots completed his ensemble. The roughness of his appearance, leather and tattoos, was the complete opposite of her silk and pearls, yet suddenly he was everything she found fascinating.

She couldn't see the other man he was talking to, but she made out a hand gesture that was all too familiar. Sign language. He'd told the big biker to stay and a second later, he turned, heading into the waiting room. Her gaze met his and he halted. They stared at each other, and Kaiya had the sense of free falling, although she knew she hadn't moved. His honey-colored eyes contrasted sharply with his tan face. A day's growth of stubble lined his cheeks and chin, adding a tough texture to his countenance. He wasn't conventionally handsome by any means. His features were a little too wide, his nose a little too crooked from being obviously broken once or twice. A scar ran down the left side of his face, dissecting his eyebrow but thankfully missing his eye. Yet, there was something about him that drew her. Maybe it was the sorrow and rage trapped in those eyes that spoke to her — two emotions she knew all too well.

He sat next to her, and although he kept his gaze trained away, she couldn't help but stare at him. He was big and slouched in the chair to rest his head against the back of it. Maybe to keep from looking at her? Kaiya didn't know for sure. A tattoo crawled up the side of his neck, originating from below his collar. The word *LIVE* lined his fingers between the first and second knuckles, and she wondered what word graced his other hand. Maybe it was just the bad-boy image that drew her, but she didn't care. She wanted to talk to him. Taking a deep breath, she leaned over until she was in his line of sight and signed to him.

"Hello."

He swerved his head to look at her so fast she was shocked he didn't get whiplash. She signed again.

"Hello, I'm Kaiya."

He studied her face, her hands, finally glancing at her ears. From the outside, she knew she looked like a perfect little doll. Makeup expertly applied. Hair flawlessly coiffed. She wore expensive, impeccable clothes. No one knew her inside didn't match her outside, not even close. Even Chloe assumed she was just a beautiful shell. Everyone saw only what he or she wanted to see, not bothering to notice that deep inside resided a dark and restless woman.

The man straightened and brought his hands up in front of himself. She caught the word *RIDE* on his other set of fingers, and tingly feelings shot through her. She stared at his big hands, waiting.

Finally, he signed back. "I am Gabby."

She smiled at him. He was slow, which meant he was out of practice, but knowing they could communicate eased the tightness in her chest. She never got the opportunity to talk to someone who wasn't part of her grandfather's world, and for the past year, all she'd been doing was practicing her Japanese sign language. She'd grown up using the American version, and much preferred it.

"Are you visiting someone in the hospital?" she asked.

He shook his head. "My president's woman was shot."

Kaiya cocked her head. "My cousin was shot. Chloe."

"Yes. Chloe," he responded. He cocked his head. "You're the new accountant?"

"I don't know," she signed. "All I know is that Chloe requested me to come to Bair. I am an accountant, though."

He stared at her hands in confusion then looked up at her. He spoke. "I'm rusty at sign. I don't know what you just said."

She read his lips and nodded, letting him know that she understood. She slowed her hand motions.

"I am not sure."

He made the universal sign of okay.

Gabby turned his head toward the doorway, and she followed his line of sight to see her grandfather standing there. Like always, a cold hand squeezed her insides whenever he was around. She might have hated living in Japan, but at least she'd been five thousand miles away from *him*. Hiro Matsumoto glanced from her to Gabby and back again. Disapproval turned his features into a sour frown. Oh yes, she was quite familiar with that look.

"You are now in the employ of Romeo Barrigan," her grandfather signed. "If you wish to decline the work, come with me."

Shock swarmed through her, and she blinked, unsure if she'd only imagined the freedom that he offered. Chloe had always been protective of her, ever since she'd gone deaf at the age of ten. What had her cousin given their grandfather in order to get him to let her go?

"Do you wish to stay or leave?" he demanded.

Kaiya got to her feet to face him. "I wish to stay."

Her grandfather drew his shoulders back, causing him to stand ramrod straight. "If you do this, I will not protect you anymore."

She bowed at the waist, showing respect. When she stood again, she signed, "I understand."

Weariness appeared in Hiro's eyes, causing the fine lines around them to tighten. He suddenly seemed to age right there, looking far older than his seventy some years. "Chloe will need someone to take care of her until she is on her feet again. I am unsure if these men are able to perform that task."

"I will help her."

He opened his mouth as if to say something, but a second later, closed it just as fast. He flexed his jaw angrily.

She held his stare unflinchingly.

"*Sayounara*, Kaiya."

Although he had spoken it aloud, she understood him. She bowed again, then he was gone, walking swiftly away while flanked by two lackeys. Hiro Matsumoto wasn't a good man. He'd made many enemies over the years, so his need for bodyguards was constant, even in the small town of Bair.

Gabby tapped her shoulder to get her attention and she read his lips.

"So you *are* our new accountant," he said.

"So it seems," she signed. Knowing that she wouldn't be returning to Japan caused happiness to bubble up inside her. "I am free."

"You weren't free before?"

She shook her head. Then she grinned, and she knew she probably looked like a crazy woman, but for the first time in a very long time, the shackles constricting her broke free. She felt…limitless.

"I've just received a get out of jail card," she signed.

Gabby chuckled. Or at least, she saw that he did. She couldn't hear him, of course, and a small pang hit her heart that she'd never know what his laughter sounded like.

He broke off when another person entered the waiting room. Kaiya felt his presence and turned to see a man dressed similar to Gabby with the same leather jacket and cautious expression. His short hair was just as dark, and he stared at her intently. She realized this must be the man he'd been talking to earlier. He didn't seem as hard-edged as Gabby, but that didn't make him any less tough or dangerous. His gaze met hers, and again, she had a sense that she'd just met her destiny. Fanciful, perhaps, but maybe it was time for her to believe in fairy tales again.

Chapter Two

"You had something to do with this, didn't you?" Kaiya asked, speaking aloud to her cousin. Chloe was the only person she talked to. Since she couldn't hear herself speak, she had no idea how her voice sounded, although she suspected she sounded like a screeching hyena.

Her cousin lay in a hospital bed, surrounded by machines hooked up to her in one place or another. Kaiya couldn't hear the beeps and whistles, but at least all the graphs and numbers suggested Chloe was doing well.

"Boone will help you get started," Chloe signed. Since her lung had collapsed, it was a good thing she didn't have to talk and waste breath.

"I met Boone in the lobby. And Gabby. I like them."

Chloe smiled. "I like them too."

"Good. You almost died for one of them."

Chloe shrugged. "The Men of Hell are my family now. I want them to be your family too."

"Family. That would be nice, considering we haven't had that in a while. What did you give Grandfather to get me away from him?"

"I forgave him."

Kaiya closed her eyes. For her cousin to grant *that* humbled Kaiya in a profound way. She might have been a doll all her life, but Chloe had fought tooth and nail against the rage and darkness inside her.

"Thank you, cousin."

Chloe took hold of her hand and squeezed. "You can live your life now, Kaiya. It's what I've always wanted for you."

* * * *

Visiting hours were short because Chloe still needed around the clock care, and as Kaiya left the room, she saw Romeo and Dax waiting for their turn to say goodnight. It had been over a year since Romeo had helped rescue her from being kidnapped, but he looked exactly as she remembered him. From her purse, she pulled out her notebook and pen, the one she kept ready for moments just like this.

"Thank you," she wrote and held it up for him to see.

"For what?" he asked.

She wrote more. "For saving me. For loving her."

"For saving you, you're welcome. For loving her, well, Chloe's hard *not* to love."

She smiled and nodded, then she went to walk past them when Dax held out a hand to halt her. She looked at him inquiringly.

"Where are you staying?"

She shrugged. A big hand pressed against her back, and before she even looked, her sixth sense told her it had to be either Gabby or Boone. Her heart rate sped

15

up at the idea of either of them being near her, and her belly quivered with excitement. She glanced up. Boone stood behind her.

"She'll stay at the clubhouse," he said, catching her gaze and holding her, mesmerized.

Something electric arched between them.

"Gabby and I will take her back."

She wasn't aware of anything else as Boone pressed his hand over her lower spine and guided her away from her cousin's hospital room. The heat of his hand burned through her clothing, warming her—turning her on. She'd had sex before, in a concentrated effort to be normal, but she hadn't enjoyed it. Probably because she hadn't had someone arouse her with a single touch. Something told her Boone and Gabby were different and would know the right way to handle her, make her scream with passion. Oh, they were still dangerous, still had that cold streak that ran in their eyes and a roughness that only living a tough life could instill. The way they moved, the way they studied everything around them showed they had grit and strength that couldn't be faked.

In contrast, she couldn't have been more different. A fraud. She'd been sheltered from a young age, made worse when she'd gotten sick and lost her hearing. She was tall, reed thin and weak. The complete opposite of Chloe, of these men, of their lifestyle. But she had lots of kinky ideas she'd love to play out. If she dealt her cards right, she may just have found two men to help her live out the fantasies she'd gathered from her beloved books.

Boone didn't stop at the waiting room. Gabby met them, and they left the hospital together, walking out in the cool evening air. A row of motorcycles sat lined up in the parking lot, and a few bikers in leather and chains stood around smoking. They greeted Boone and Gabby, trained curious eyes on her.

She read each of their lips.

"Who's the chick?"

"How's Chloe?"

She didn't know what Boone and Gabby said, because she didn't look at them, but their responses must have been brief since they didn't stop. Boone guided her over to a motorcycle.

Gabby got on before he signed, "Climb on."

She eyed him dubiously. "Behind you?"

Gabby nodded. "Trust us, Kaiya."

She took a deep breath and decided now was as good of a time as any to let loose. She wanted to find out if the vibration of a motorcycle between her legs would really stimulate her clit like she'd read.

With Boone's help, she learned how to mount the bike and where to put her feet. He handed her a helmet, which slipped too far over her forehead to be comfortable, but at least she had some protection. A few seconds later, the big machine rumbled to life between her thighs. Good God! It *was* a gigantic vibrator. The reverberations echoed up through her sex and she rolled her hips forward a little to press her clit firmly against the seat. She wrapped her arms around Gabby's waist, and he looked over his shoulder to smirk at her as if he knew what she'd done. Kaiya didn't care. As they sped through the parking lot with a thunderous roar, Kaiya couldn't help but gasp with sheer pleasure.

Her expensive pantsuit did nothing to fend off the cool night wind, but she'd be damned if she'd complain. The ride exhilarated her, her heart thumping with excitement and her blood pumping with endorphins. The air rushing by was a freedom all in itself. She was terrified and thrilled all at the same time, like jumping out of a plane without a parachute. Only she knew she was safe. Gabby was with her and Boone rode next to them. Not caring who heard her twisted version of a voice, she laughed.

They flew past the interstate and headed toward farmland. The rows of corn zoomed by so fast that they looked like rippling water. Then all too quickly, the ride ended, and Kaiya got her first glimpse of her new home. At first, she thought she was right back in prison again. High concrete walls surrounded the place. Turrets held men who surveyed the perimeters. But once they entered, the warm lights of the house beckoned them closer, although the bullet holes in the wood had her wondering about safety. Men smiled and waved. A campfire with men sitting around drinking beer looked inviting.

Gabby drove the bike into a garage and shut down the thrilling stimulation, much to her disappointment. He helped her off the motorcycle. She wobbled due to quivering knees and unsteady legs. The bike ride had done more to her body than just exciting her. He hauled her in close to his body, keeping her from falling. The overhead light bulb gave off a muted, sickly glow, but it was enough to see the desire in Gabby's honey-colored eyes. An answering need throbbed through her pussy, shocking her. She'd only had sex with two men in the past, men who had worked for her grandfather, and neither one of them had ever made her juices run like she'd read in the romance books. The chemistry between her, Gabby and Boone, however, made her think she was finally going to know how fulfilling sex could be. Before she could blink, Gabby covered her lips with his. Her thoughts scattered to the wind when he ran his tongue across the seam and she parted her mouth. He plundered her depths, and she moaned at the fire that licked through her. His grip on her hips tightened and he bent her back slightly as he rubbed his hard cock against the spot that still tingled from the motorcycle ride. She gripped his shoulders, needing something to hold onto. Thick cords of muscles bulged under her hands. He was big and solid and so damn hot he made her burn. When he broke the kiss to trail small kisses across her cheek, she drew in great gulps of air. Oh, yes. This was it. This excitement was what she'd been searching for.

Slowly, he pulled back and took her hand. She had to bite back a groan of frustration since she wanted more, but apparently, he had other ideas. He led her from the garage toward the house and Boone waited for them at the door. The smirk on his face told her he'd seen the kiss. She probably should have been embarrassed, but she wasn't. That kiss had been the equivalent of a nuclear bomb blowing her dormant life apart, and she resolved to experience it again.

Soon.

* * * *

Gabby adjusted his dick in his now too-tight jeans. He caught Boone's knowing look but ignored his friend as he marched into the clubhouse. Men and club whores filled the den, getting it on. Heavy metal music blared from speakers, the thumping a bit too loud to be comfortable. He grimaced. He couldn't hear in one ear because of trauma, and he didn't relish losing the other side because of acoustics. He stepped up to the bar and gestured for a beer. The prospect behind the counter handed him a cold bottle. Kaiya stepped forward from the shadowy doorway, and one by one, the men stopped what they were doing to study her. He had to admit her silk clothes and doll-like features looked out of place among the leather and chains that were the normal attire. She smiled at everyone as if she personally knew each of them, and damn if his dick didn't get harder at how beautiful she was. Boone stood behind her, his hand in the small of her back, his protective stance marking his territory. Gabby felt something dark twist inside him. They'd just met and already there was an easy vibe between her and Boone that Gabby knew he'd never feel. He wasn't a soft or kind man, which was what Kaiya deserved. Hell, he'd known her for five seconds and could already tell she was a lady with a capital L. The silk covering her body was a neon sign blasting her refinery. He shouldn't have kissed her. Christ, one taste and he wanted more. He turned away from the sight of Boone and Kaiya standing close, drained his beer and gestured for another.

A small hand slid over his shoulder, and his libido went into overdrive. No club pussy had ever caused such a fire in his body. Gabby turned. Kaiya stood next to him, head cocked with a tiny smile gracing her lips. His heart thumped heavily at her nearness. He may not be the right man for her, but damned if he cared about doing the right thing.

"Will you and Boone show me around?" she signed.

He glanced at Boone before looking at the men who stared at them as if they were some type of interesting *telenovela*. Fucking Burrito got most of the men hooked on his favorite show, even though no one else spoke Spanish. Well, guess his secret was about to be revealed. He sighed.

"Sure," he signed back. The more he practiced with her, the more he remembered. "I suppose you'll be staying here while Chloe is in the hospital?"

She nodded. "Yes, if that's okay with the club."

He thought he heard someone say something, but the music drowned out the words. He glared at the speaker, and suddenly the sound died, leaving a roaring of silence in his one good ear. He frowned at Boone.

"You know sign language, Gabby?" Hook asked.

Gabby turned his head so his good ear could hear anything else asked. As soon as he figured out Kaiya would be at the club, he knew the questions would be coming. He nodded.

"He's deaf in one ear," Boone replied.

He shot his friend a dark look.

Boone ignored him. "So let's try to keep the acoustics at non-lethal decibels."

Kaiya touched his arm again, and when he looked at her, she signed, "Introduce me?"

Christ!

He rose and pointed to the first man he saw.

"Hook," he said in sign.

The man waved. On the back of his hand shone a gleaming silver hook tattoo, extending from his cuff and touching his knuckles, which explained how he'd gotten his nickname.

Gabby added, "He has a thing for Peter Pan."

Kaiya smiled widely at Hook.

"What did you tell her about me?" Hook demanded.

Gabby ignored him and went down the line. Sioux, Burrito, Marcus. With each name, she smiled at the man and held out her hand to shake. Truth be known, he didn't like her touching other men and clenched his fists in an effort not to grab her and haul her away from them. Shit, he'd just met her and now he was thinking like a damn caveman.

"Kaiya is our new accountant," Boone announced.

"And new pussy?" Marcus asked.

Boone shook his head. "She's Chloe's cousin and a part of this club, so that makes her off limits. Hear me?"

"You claiming her?" Sioux asked. He ran an insolent eye up and down her body. Gabby tensed and took a step closer to Kaiya, making sure the man lost his interest right away. Sioux held up a hand. "Understood, Brother."

He glared at each in turn. Hell, he knew he was no good for her, but he'd be damned if he allowed any of the other yahoos to think they could lay a hand on her. Never before had this type of protectiveness surged through him, and he wasn't sure how to handle it. He looked toward Boone for help.

"Come on," Boone said, reading Gabby's lost expression.

Boone always had his back, for which he was grateful. There wasn't anyone he trusted like he did Boone, and he didn't like to think how his life would've turned out had he not had Boone's support.

Boone led them from the den of ill repute and Gabby gestured for Kaiya to follow. He trailed after her, tossing another fierce look at the men. Yes, he trusted them with his life, but not around fresh pussy.

Boone led her into the back, past Romeo's office to the room that used to be Cipher's workspace. The last accountant had been skimming the books, and Romeo had taught him a lesson he'd never forget. Kaiya walked into the area and stared at the mess scattered about. Ledger books, opened and closed, lined every surface. Receipts and pieces of papers lay in haphazard piles. The trash can overflowed and the ashtray stank with stubbed-out butts.

"I didn't realize how bad this place was," Boone mused.

Gabby threw him a glare. He got Kaiya's attention. "I'll clean this up."

"No need," she signed back. "I need to create my own working environment."

"Tell her she can have Cipher's old bedroom," Boone said to Gabby.

"Tell him I can read his lips," Kaiya signed.

Gabby looked at Boone. "She can read lips, you know."

Boone flushed and rubbed the back of his neck. "Noted. I promise not to be so obtuse in the future."

She nodded and looked at Gabby. "I thought he knew sign."

"He knows the basics. Hi. Sit. Stay. All that's missing is a pat on the head."

She grinned then turned back to the cluttered office. Yeah, Gabby knew without her signing a word that she had her work cut out for her.

Chapter Three

Three days later…

Kaiya sat up straight and rolled her head. Little pops went off, easing the tension a bit. She was tired, hungry and had a slight headache from hunching over the books. This Cipher person had done one hell of a job fucking up the Men of Hell, because she'd finally discovered that on top of fleecing the club, he'd also been stealing from this so-called Master as well. She was still trying to piece together his shorthand.

As she stretched, she caught movement out of the corner of her eye and turned. Gabby leaned in the doorway, ankles crossed, arms folded over his chest as he watched her. Perhaps his intense stare should've creeped her out, but it simply turned her on—a lot. She really was going to have to do something about her attraction sooner rather than later.

"You need to eat," he signed.

She shook her head. "I'm not hungry. Besides, these books are a mess."

"The books can wait for a bit. I want you to eat, Kaiya."

Logically, she knew he didn't mean anything more than that he was concerned about her, but his words still rubbed her the wrong way. Too many times her grandfather had said the exact same thing—'I want you to eat, Kaiya'—only his words had held a promise of retribution if she didn't comply. Usually, something was taken away or withheld, like her precious books.

"Do *not* tell me what to do!" she signed angrily.

He raised an eyebrow. "I'm not telling you what to do. I'm reminding you that you need to eat."

She shook her head stubbornly.

He cocked his head at her. "What's the matter with you?"

The matter with *her*? When he was trying to take over her free will? The more she remembered the past, the more her simmering anger built until it flashed like lightning. It shot through her, burning so hot she didn't even realize what she was doing until her fists thumped against his chest. He reacted quickly, securing her arms and preventing her from moving. For a moment, the crushing weight of being trapped had terror slicing through her body, until Gabby rubbed his cheek against her temple in a soothing gesture. Just as quickly as her rage had boiled over, it cooled, and she was left staring up in shock at Gabby's calm face.

"Stop acting like a child," he said.

She suspected his tone was stern.

"I'm not telling you what to do, Kaiya."

Kaiya read his lips and pulled away to hug herself. What had come over her? Perhaps she *was* too stressed and tired from scrutinizing the ledgers. Shame had her bowing her head.

"I'm sorry," she signed. "I don't know why I did that. I've never hit anyone before."

He used a finger to lift her chin. "I hope you know I'd never force you to do anything you don't want to do."

She read his words and nodded.

"Kaiya, you've been holed up in this room for three days straight," he continued, doing a mixture of speaking and signing. "It's not healthy."

He was right. She'd even slept in here, hunched over her desk. Kaiya raised her arm, smelled her armpit and grimaced. The mystery of what Cipher had done had become an addiction.

"All right," she signed. "I need to clean up and I will come to dinner."

He smiled, although most would consider his smile more predatory than humorous. It made the scar on his face twist into something fierce and dangerous looking, but all it did was immediately turn on her libido. How could she have ignored both Gabby and Boone like that? He took her hand in his and escorted her up the stairs.

Her luggage had arrived and was stored into Cipher's old bedroom. Kaiya had yet to use the bed. The first time she'd been in there, the room had smelled like moldy gym shorts and cigarettes, so she'd opened the window to air it out. Now, it wasn't that smelly, but the filth still lingered. One reason she'd slept at her desk was that she couldn't imagine sleeping on the sheets, especially since she had no idea what'd happened on them before her arrival. Living the past three days in the clubhouse, she'd seen *lots* of things. And positions. She pursed her lips. There probably wasn't a place that hadn't been used for sex. What a difference between where she'd come from and here. The lack of cleanliness might have been a bit disturbing but what had caused it all was a turn-on as well. Maybe she should buy some toys.

Would Boone and Gabby mind using a dildo on me?

The question brought lascivious thoughts to mind, like being one of the people getting it on out in plain sight. There were many fantasies she wanted to explore. Perhaps it was time to put her work into perspective and tear her prim little doll image to shreds.

* * * *

One week later…

Her office was finally starting to show some semblance of order. The room smelled like lemon furniture polish, the trash had been taken out and the ashtrays removed. The carpet had been vacuumed within an inch of its life. She even had one of those scented plug-ins to give the room a little more perfume.

On the floor rested her unmarked box of toys she had yet to carry to her bedroom. She sighed. She really ought to move that away, just in case someone thought to open it. No doubt, they'd probably steal the contents for themselves. How embarrassing it would be to see some of them men using the toys she'd bought for herself.

Right next to the box were rows of neat stacks of papers, stuff she had to sift through carefully to figure out what they were. Her grandfather had several accountants, each doing their best to put a legitimate spin on the illegal activities that made Hiro Matsumoto a very wealthy man. He had often forgotten how she could read lips, and his men had talked freely. She'd learned from the best. She was positive she could make the Men of Hell look as though rose petals floated out of their asses. First, however, she had to uncover the little mystery Cipher had left behind. The books didn't make sense, but if there was one thing Kaiya never backed away from, it was a challenge.

Boone appeared at her door, and she smiled at him, gesturing for him to come in. It had been almost two weeks since she'd arrived, and in that time, the three of them had talked. Somewhat. Stilted conversations and her focus on the books hadn't helped them learn about one another. Regret flashed through her. She'd hoped they'd be sharing a bed by now.

"Hello, Kaiya," Boone said. He strolled in and sat on one of the folding chairs.

She read his lips and picked up a notebook and pen. "Hi," she wrote.

He smiled, showing a little teeth and a lot of charm. He gave her a heated look through the fan of his lashes, and she wondered how long he'd practiced that devilish come-hither look. It was working. That smile should be outlawed because she had the wildest urge to shuck her panties and jump onto his lap. Instead, she bit her lower lip to hold down her lascivious daydreams.

"I was wondering if you'd like to go out to dinner with me and Gabby."

She blinked, a little surprised. Gabby was not a very social person. Before she could answer yes, however, he continued.

"I want you to know right off that Gabby and I are partners. You don't just date one of us. You'll be dating both of us."

She cocked one of eyebrow and scribbled on the paper, "You are lovers?"

When he read that, his eyes widened in surprise. "Ah, no. Not *that* type of partner. We're Brothers but…more than club Brothers. We served together in the Marines. He, ah, saved my life."

"Is that how he got his scar?"

Boone nodded. "And where he lost his hearing. It's…my fault. I owe him everything."

He shifted in his seat uneasily. The way he drummed his fingers on the outer edge of his thigh and how he constantly checked the perimeter of the room suggested there was probably a whole lot more to the story, but she didn't want to push. One thing she understood more than anyone else was the need for privacy. After she'd lost her hearing, her parents had forced her to a therapist to share her feelings and emotions on what had happened. Kaiya had hated every minute of it. Her time sitting in a chair to tell some stranger how devastated she'd become was tantamount to raping her mind, in her opinion. No one could understand her loss and just talking about it only made it worse. Some things were better left unexplored.

"So when I say we're partners, well, I take care of Gabby," he clarified. "There are certain residual aftereffects of our time in war that still haunt him."

"You take care of him out of guilt?" she asked.

"I take care of him because he's my friend."

She smiled, liking his answer.

"I understand," she wrote. "Truthfully, I never pictured one of you without the other. Of course, I'd love to go to dinner with both of you. When?"

"Tonight," he said. "Chloe comes home from the hospital tomorrow, so I know your time is going to be limited."

True. Chloe had opted out of a rehabilitation hospital, so Kaiya had volunteered to help with her physical therapy. Romeo and Dax had offered, but they were so busy rebuilding the clubhouse that she didn't see how they'd have time to devote to her cousin's complete recovery.

"Okay."

He read her simple note and smiled. When he rose from the chair, her breath caught. The man was simply divine. Big, muscular, hard in all the right places, if the fit of his clothes were any indication. One particular hardness pressing against the inside of his jeans held her attention, clearly showing how endowed he was. Her mouth salivated.

Boone laid his fists on the desk and leaned forward. Kaiya leaned toward him as well, and centered her gaze on his lips.

"Wear jeans, pretty lady," he said. "You'll be...riding."

The innuendo was unmistakable. Her heart thundered wildly in her chest. In the few times she'd had sex, she'd *never* been this turned on. This kind of anticipation was even better than the foreplay in her naughty novels.

Boone winked at her, as if he knew exactly what she was thinking and feeling, then he turned to leave. She kept her gaze glued on his perfectly sculptured ass encased in well-worn jeans. Kaiya had half a mind to put her fingers to her pussy and bring herself to orgasm. Then she remembered the goodies in the box and grabbed it before hurrying from her office. She closed the door behind her with a sharp click but didn't lock it in case Romeo wanted to look over her progress, although she figured no one would miss her for ten or fifteen minutes.

In her bedroom, she turned the lock on the door and hurried to her newly acquired toys. She didn't waste a second, pulling out the big pink vibrator. She opened the package, washed the thing off and inserted the batteries. Lying on the bed, she lifted her skirt and shimmied out of her panties, noting that the encounter with Boone had made her wet.

Closing her eyes, Kaiya flicked on the vibrator, pressed it to her pussy and let her imagination fly. She pictured Boone and Gabby standing at the edge of the bed, watching as she pleasured herself, swollen cocks in their hands as they pumped the shafts. Droplets of perspiration ran down her skin, soaking the sheets beneath her as she fucked herself with the vibrator. There were so many kinky things she wanted to try, and being watched was one of them. Thighs wide, she used her free hand to rub her clitoris, moving her fingers in erotic little circles. She paused every so often to suck the juice from her fingers, relishing the taste of herself. She interspersed light movement with harder, faster rubbing. Her body began to twitch as the first tiny electrical pulses radiated out from her throbbing clit. Her head remained filled with the image of Boone and Gabby watching her, jacking off with her, moaning their approval of such base desires, tugging on their cocks as they called her dirty names — cunt, whore. Yes, she *was* a dirty little slut.

Gabby and Boone would come, bliss covering their faces as they ejaculated, showering her face and breasts with thick spurts of cum. Kaiya slammed her thighs shut over the toy just as a shattering orgasm ripped through her. She convulsed, shuddering from head to toe as vise-like contractions clamped her pussy around the vibrator.

She lay panting, trying to gather her scattered wits. Her body was satisfied for now, but it left a simmering need for her two men. Good thing she was going on a date with them later.

Chapter Four

Kaiya rubbed her sweating palms along her jeans and took deep breaths in an effort to slow her racing heart. She never thought she'd be this nervous. This was, technically, her first date. The two men she'd had relations with had been employees of her grandfather, and at no time did they even hint about taking her out somewhere. They'd been a dirty little secret, although she often wondered how ignorant Hiro Matsumoto had actually been. After her dalliances with the employees, it wasn't long before both men had been replaced.

She shook off the memories. It was not time to think of other men, especially her other lovers. She held no illusions that Boone and Gabby had probably fucked every pussy that slept at the club, but she didn't let it bother her. She planned to be up front with both men. If they wanted her, the three of them would be exclusive for however long their relationship lasted. If they wanted to fuck other women, she wouldn't stop them, but it would be over. She didn't play games. Well, at least not those kinds of games. She planned to do a lot of role-playing, however, with Boone and Gabby.

At seven, both men appeared in her doorway. She was going to have to get to a strobe signaler and rig it to the door somehow, but for now, she'd left it open, knowing they were going to arrive. Kaiya took a deep breath and smiled at them. Butterflies danced through her belly as Gabby held out his hand for her and she placed hers trustingly in the big palm. He led her out of the room, down the stairs and through the clubhouse with Boone following. Once again, the other members were partying. A prospect stood behind the bar serving beer. Scantily clad girls danced to music that Kaiya couldn't hear but felt through the thumping against the floor. Some were in the men's laps, kissing and grinding. The scent of sex lingered in the air, along with cigarettes, sweat and old fermentation. She was slowly getting used to the not-quite-pleasant odor.

The night air gently wafted by, so she zipped up her jacket. She had worn the jeans like Boone had suggested, and had tucked the legs into calf-high leather boots. Since she didn't own any T-shirts, she wore a cotton button-down. Gabby handed her a helmet, smaller than the one she'd used the other day. A price tag was still attached on the inside. She used her thumbnail to scrape it off. It touched her that he'd gone and bought something for her. She smiled her thanks and strapped it on. A little visor came down over her eyes.

Gabby mounted his gigantic bike. He wrangled it upward before kicking the stand back and gesturing with his head for her to climb behind him. She straddled the thing like Boone had shown her and wrapped her arms around his waist. The bike rumbled to life and off they went, leaving the compound behind.

Boone led the way as they raced down the road. She angled her hips to get the maximum benefit of being on the bike, and knew that the tease would only amp up the anticipation of what would happen after the date. No way would she settle for just a peck goodnight, not after masturbating herself into nirvana.

They didn't go very far, only to the beginning of the interstate before they pulled into a diner. Next to it stood a burned-out shell of building. Gabby pulled to a stop, and she slithered off as he cut the engine. The vibration stopped, and she missed the pulsing sensation. Boone walked up to her and took her hand to lead her inside.

It was just a plain diner, nothing spectacular, and yet, she couldn't squelch the nervous excitement of being on her first date. The hostess led them to a booth, and Kaiya slid in, with Gabby sitting across from her. Boone sat beside her.

"I know this is nothing fancy," Boone said.

She pulled out her pen and notebook from the inner pocket of her jacket. "This is great!" she wrote. "I've never been to a diner."

Both men blinked at her, looking startled.

"Did you grow up in Japan?" Gabby signed.

She shook her head and wrote, "No, I was born here. My grandfather prevented me from going to places like this. So thank you. Best date ever!"

Gabby smiled. The waitress walked up with her pen and little order pad, and the men started talking to her. Kaiya only caught half of what they were saying since she couldn't see each person's lips, but when it came time for her, she wrote down a cheeseburger, fries and a chocolate shake. She'd always wanted to try that. The waitress looked at her like she was weird, but Kaiya didn't let it bother her. People always looked at her strangely.

"How long have you been with the Men of Hell?" she wrote and held the pad up to Boone.

"Gabby and I both joined when we were discharged from the Marines," he said.

She nodded.

"Technically, I'm a disabled vet," Gabby signed. "I got wounded in battle and once I recovered, I was discharged from service."

He fingered his scar, and she noticed it was more of an absent-minded gesture than a conscious one. He pulled his brows together in a dark scowl and she surmised it was because of memories. She may not have known them long, but Kaiya had spent a lifetime studying people. Gabby Dixon didn't like reminders. He was a quiet man who kept to himself, and the words tattooed on his fingers only reinforced his need to forget. It made her wonder what type of man he would've been if he hadn't found the motorcycle club. She decided to change topics.

"I lost my hearing at age ten," she wrote on her notepad. "My parents and I went to Asia on vacation. I contracted bacterial meningitis and the doctors there treated me with ototoxic drugs. The combination left me deaf."

Both men frowned but they didn't look at her with pity. She liked that. So many times people changed when they learned about had what happened to her. They suddenly thought she was a poor *thing* instead of a woman who had gone on to receive her college degree in accounting. Gabby and Boone simply perceived her as if they were discovering one more fact, which is how she hoped this date would proceed. She wanted to know everything about these two big men.

The food arrived, and all thought of talking ended as she dug into her meal. The cheeseburger was messy but good, the French fries greasy yet tasty and the chocolate shake was simply divine. One of the best meals she'd ever eaten.

Boone touched her arm, and when she turned to face him, he grinned. "For a tiny thing you sure can put the food away."

She grabbed her pen and paper. "I'm not tiny. I'm five foot ten. Very tall for a woman."

"Yeah, but you weigh what? A hundred pounds soaking wet?"

The lines around his eyes crinkled delightfully so she knew he was simply teasing her. She decided to be a little naughty. Quickly, she wrote out a reply and as she showed it to him, she laid her hand on his upper thigh.

"If you're worried I won't be able to take your cock…don't be."

She read his lips. "Fuck me."

She nodded, letting him know that yes, she wanted to very much.

Gabby rose and headed toward the cashier. He pulled his wallet out of his back pocket and handed over some bills. Just like that, dinner was over. Boone scooted out of the booth and grabbed her hand. The two men practically raced out of the diner as if the Hounds of Hell were on their heels. Pride and power surged through her, knowing that she was able to drive these two strong men a little crazy.

This time she sat behind Boone as they raced out of the parking lot back to the compound. She couldn't appreciate the night ride with thoughts of what lay at the end of their journey — getting all hot and sweaty in a good way with the two gorgeous men. The expectation had desire pooling in her belly and trickling down to her pussy. She grew wet just thinking about how the night was going to progress.

Boone and Gabby didn't say much as they parked their bikes, then they all but dragged her off the back and through the house. At the top of the stairs, they didn't head to her small room. Instead, they turned left and marched to another room. Gabby opened the door, then it was the three of them cocooned in the darkness with the bed only a few feet away.

Boone took her mouth in a kiss, slanting his lips across hers until he forced them apart. He deepened the lip lock, caressing his tongue along hers. By the time he raised his head, she was breathless—waiting, wanting.

Gabby kissed her next, just like when they had stood next to his bike that first night. Her clothes came off in between kisses. She couldn't strip fast enough and when she was completely naked, she knelt before them and ran a hand up each of their muscular thighs—two cocks, hard as nails, outlined through the denim. This was what she wanted, to suck them both off until they shot their loads over her body and got it in her hair. That's what good little sluts did for their men. The wicked thoughts had her pussy juice flowing, and she quickly unzipped Gabby's pants before doing the same to Boone's. The men helped, pushing down their jeans and underwear until their thick dicks were revealed. Kaiya immediately encircled them with her hands, gripping both cocks that were equally big, although Gabby's might have been a little longer. Fluid appeared at the tip of each cock, spilling over. She licked one then the other, loving the salty taste of their pre-cum. She looked up at Gabby and Boone. They watched her with hooded gazes, lust making their eyes burn brightly. She scooped up new drops of their essence on her finger and, watching them, stuck out her tongue and wiped her finger clean. She couldn't hear their groans but felt the rumble in their bodies. Then she pointed to their cocks before touching her breasts, alluding to where she wanted them to aim. Both men nodded, so she went back to the blow job.

She fisted Gabby and brought her mouth down on Boone, sucking until her cheeks hollowed. He speared his fingers in her hair, guiding her up and down on his cock. At first, she went slow and steady, savoring the feel of him gliding in and out of her mouth. She'd only given one other blow job and the dick had been slim and short. Boone's cock hit her gag reflex and she couldn't help the slight closing of her throat. He instantly stilled and tried to pull away, but she held his hips. She had to adapt quickly and relax her throat muscles as well as breathe out of her nose, and she learned that he really liked when she swallowed around his cockhead.

After a moment, Kaiya pulled off and changed positions, this time swallowing Gabby while giving Boone the hand job. Gabby felt slightly different in her mouth—more robust. His pre-cum was a little more potent. Instead of continuing the leisurely exploration as she'd done with Boone, Kaiya sucked him with quick, bobbing actions. She made sure to use her tongue in the slit every time she came down to capture whatever fluid came out of the tip.

Then she pulled off him to continue on Boone. Back and forth she went, loving the taste of each. Her clit tingled, her pussy ached, and she wanted to feel them jacking all over her. Deciding to focus on one, she sucked Boone down and worked him until he tensed and tried to pull out of her mouth. She backed away and gave him a hand job until he squirted his jizz on her tits.

Watching him come on her skin made her feel dirty —
wanton. She loved how the act seemed like it belonged
in a cheap motel and wished she could hear his moans
of pleasure. Once Boone was finished, he sat on the bed,
casually stroking his deflating cock while she turned
her attention to Gabby. Their gazes met as she
worshiped him on her knees, and he buried his fingers
in her hair. At first, he guided her, much as Boone had,
until she relaxed and let him take over.

She looked up at him from her kneeling position, her
head back as he fucked her mouth, allowing them to
stare at each another. She gripped his thighs, holding
on, loving the rush as he pistoned his cock in and out
of her mouth. She gave him permission to use her in
such a base way as to let her fantasy play out. He
pumped faster, and when he pulled out of her mouth,
she closed her eyes and leaned back to let him shoot
where he wanted. A splash of warm cum hit her face,
her neck, across her breasts. Just picturing herself
draped in their spunk turned her on so much that she
slipped a finger into the folds of her pussy.

Boone removed her hand, then picked her up and laid
her on the bed. He buried his face between her thighs,
licking her from the bottom of her slit to the top. When
he sucked her needy clit into his mouth, she couldn't
hold back her lusty cry. He ran his fingers up and down
her opening then pushed in. He fucked her with his
finger and with his mouth, unrelenting, until she burst
apart with a climax that was off the chart. She soared to
the heavens and touched the stars. As great as her self-
induced orgasm from earlier had been, this was a
hundred times better.

They all laid next to each other, with her in the
middle. The bed was barely big enough for the three of

them, but somehow, it just made it that much more intimate.

"I hope no one heard me," she signed. "I never use my voice."

Gabby took her hand and squeezed it.

Boone leaned up on an elbow and looked down at her. "Are you on birth control?"

She nodded. She used it to regulate her periods, but she didn't offer that information.

"I want us to get tested," he said. She read his lips and a little thrill shot through her. "The next time we're all together, I want to feel that tight little pussy bare against my cock. Is that all right with you?"

She made the universal sign of okay. She might even wear a butt plug so she could really live out her fantasies.

Chapter Five

The next few weeks were completely overwhelming, and Kaiya didn't get a chance to be alone with Boone and Gabby again. She found herself immersed in the biker world, dealing with club money as well as working with Romeo over a budget, as funny as that sounded. But members had to be paid, bribes had to be sent, dues had to be collected, not to mention dealing with the insurance agency over the lost bar. She had to set up a whole new system. And because Cipher had screwed them over, she wanted Romeo to know every step she took. Gabby usually sat in on their meetings so he could translate because she simply couldn't write everything down that needed explaining.

When she wasn't working on the books, or the mystery of Cipher's missing money, she worked with Chloe on the rehabilitation. The arduous therapy, which seemed easy to Kaiya but had her cousin struggling, brought them closer together. It gave them time to talk and reminisce, and move past the controlling shadow of their grandfather. It had been a long time since she'd last seen Chloe, and she was glad to see her so happy. The past finally seemed to be easing from Chloe's shoulders so happiness could shine through her darkness.

Boone and Gabby usually came to see her in her office, bringing food or something to drink, but they hadn't repeated what had happened in their room. The anticipation of having them both was a fantasy stuck on replay in her mind. Would they take her together? One at a time? The Kama Sutra might be an ancient Hindu text, but damned if she didn't want to try some of those delicious positions. She should probably start stretching to be a little more limber.

The perfect opportunity came when Chloe suggested Kaiya go live in a member's old house. Chloe seemed stagnated on the idea that the clubhouse was too rough and rowdy for her, and she only agreed to look at the house so Chloe wouldn't be upset. One afternoon—technically during her lunch break although Romeo always told her to take however long she wanted—Kaiya stared at a brick, ranch-style house before her. The only drawback she could see to living here was not being close to Gabby and Boone all the time and she wasn't sure if she liked the distance.

"You should be resting," she signed to Chloe as they walked closer to the house. Upon further inspection, the yard was a bit overgrown and in desperate need of weed trimming.

"And you need to be out of the clubhouse," her cousin said.

Kaiya read her lips and saw the mutinous expression on Chloe's face. She knew that look. Once Chloe got her mind stuck on an idea, she rarely ever let it go.

Chloe put the key in the lock and turned the knob. The door swished open and the stale air inside the house rushed out to greet them. She scrunched her nose up when the stench of mothballs assaulted her. A decorator's nightmare stared back at her, with bric-a-brac lining every surface inside. She couldn't even tell what color the walls were painted because of all the stuff hanging on all conceivable areas. She sighed a bit dramatically. More cleaning. More organizing. It was almost enough to make her say 'hell, no' right then and there.

Chloe nudged her and pointed. A second later, the vibrations of four bike engines rumbled under her feet as Romeo, Dax, Gabby and Boone appeared. Kaiya's gaze landed on the two men she considered hers, both looking so damn handsome it should be illegal. They wore half-helmets and sunglasses, tattoos peeking from under their black leathers. The power and command they had on their bikes made her clit throb with impatience. Her panties irritated her sensitive pussy lips.

"You are in a relationship with two men," Kaiya said to her cousin in sign.

Chloe frowned. "Yeah. So?"

"Do you think Boone and Gabby are open to the same arrangement?"

"What?" Chloe asked sharply. "Why?"

"Because I want them." She didn't add that she'd already had them, in a way. One taste and she was hooked for however long this attraction would last.

Chloe blinked, for once at a loss for words. Her mouth opened and closed a few times, as she seemed to struggle to say something. "Uh, do you know what it means to be with two men, sweetie?"

Kaiya arched her eyebrows. "I'm not a virgin, although I think you think I am."

Chloe opened her mouth to say something but at that moment, all the men angled closer, effectively shutting down whatever she'd been about to say. Romeo and Dax couldn't read sign, but Boone was catching up fast. Chloe's men swarmed around her, leaving Kaiya to face Gabby and Boone.

"We need to talk," Gabby signed.

Kaiya gestured to the open house. "Want to talk in there?"

Boone nodded and turned to say something to the other group. Kaiya couldn't see what was said, but Gabby took her hand and led her inside. Boone joined them and flipped on the light as he closed the door. Kaiya stepped dead in her tracks. The place was worse than she'd thought. Everything from taxidermy to collectable dolls had to be on display throughout the house. It was a hoarder's wet dream. Anything that could hold an object had something collecting dust, and she sneezed. Jesus, she didn't have allergies but knew a giant bowling ball of allergens rushed toward her ready to say hello.

"Holy shit," Boone said. He pulled up the window blinds then opened the glass. Even though that helped stir the dust particles, it also managed to clear the air a little.

"This place is a mess," Gabby signed.

"I would use a more descriptive adjective," she replied. "Chaos. Mayhem. Or a fucking disaster. Take your pick."

Gabby grinned.

The rest of the house wasn't any better as the same decorating scheme continued through the whole place. She bit her lip as the dead, stuffed animals stared accusingly at her through glass eyes. The three of them ended up in the master bedroom and saw that someone had at least covered all the furniture with clear plastic.

Boone touched her shoulder, and she looked up at him.

"It's not so bad," he said.

She arched an eyebrow at him in disbelief. He shrugged and began pulling the tarps onto the floor, exposing the rich wood of the furnishings. The large bed didn't have sheets but the thick mattress looked new.

"If I move here, I won't see you both all that much," she signed.

Gabby took her hand and they sat on the bed.

"Boone and I have talked," he said. "We would come every night and visit with you. If you'd want us to."

She had expected them to move in with her, but as she searched Gabby's eyes, a darkness moved through those honey-colored orbs. He'd shut her out, and it hurt.

"Why have you not come to me?" she signed, looking back and forth between Gabby and Boone. "Was I only a one-night stand?"

"No," Gabby said. "Privacy."

She read the words and cocked her head, wanting them to explain. Boone tapped her shoulder and she looked at him.

"What we don't want, Kaiya, is an audience," Boone replied. "We want you to scream your head off without being self-conscious. So I suggested this house to Chloe for you to use."

"For *us* to use," Gabby stressed, gesturing between them.

It touched her heart that they thought of her discomposure. She remembered how to talk, remembered how to form words, but not being able to hear the words made her uncomfortable. They rumbled from her chest, discordant vibrations that had no other sound except to spill forth as unheard memories. Chloe had told her once, back when they were teenagers, that she sounded like a screeching baboon underwater and ever since then, she'd remained silent around people she didn't know all that well. Her vocalization of the pleasure they'd given her had surprised her.

As she looked in their eyes, the predatory glint was back. Tingles ran up and down her arms. Her nipples pebbled and her pussy flooded, all from the sudden hunger than surged through her body. She hadn't worn the butt plug she'd bought because she hadn't known that they were going to christen the house immediately. Still, there was a lot they could do to one another.

"I got my test results," she signed. "I'm clean."

Gabby nodded. "So are we."

"And we've not touched any of the sweet butts since we first met you," Boone said.

That was all she needed to hear. She grabbed the front of Gabby's cut and yanked him closer so she could fasten her mouth on his. Some might call her foolish for trusting them without seeing the proof, but in the month and a half since she'd been with the club, she had learned that both men were forthright and honest to a fault. Sure, they were big and dangerous, and she had no doubt they wouldn't hesitate to use the nine mils fastened under their cuts. But they were also loyal and protective, and she'd been adopted into the club family.

She pulled back, took a deep breath and brought up her hands. "I have a confession."

Gabby quirked an eyebrow.

"I have fantasies." She waited until Gabby told Boone what she said.

Although Boone was getting better, probably from the YouTube videos on sign language he'd been watching, there were still some words he didn't know.

"I have fantasies of sex being kinky and dirty, and I'm a bad, bad girl. I want you both to help me live them out."

Gabby cupped her face and kissed her hard on the mouth, promising without words that she'd be pleasured in every way that she desired. When he pulled back, she looked at his lips.

"Baby, I can be as dirty as you want me to be."

Happiness slammed through her. It was a relief that she'd found two men who didn't mind letting her play out sexual scenes in a controlled environment. She rose from the bed and faced them. Then she undressed as both men watched with fire in their eyes and hard dicks swelling in the crotch of their jeans.

Since she knew the size of their dicks, they would fill her up nice and tight, squeezing into her cunt until they hit her womb. She'd never felt that, had only read that it could be painful, but she wanted that pain. She wanted every single delicious inch of them stuffed inside her, pounding out their orgasm until their spunk ran down her thighs. The thought alone was enough to make her pussy clench in anticipation.

Once her top hit the floor, she stood there for a long moment, letting them look at her. She had small breasts. When she cupped them, they filled her palms. Her areolas were large and a dusky rose color. She pinched the nipples until they were both fully erect. Her moistened undies were next. She quickly shimmied them over her hips, down her legs then stepped out of them.

She had shaved her pussy, leaving a neatly trimmed landing strip, and planned to find a waxing center soon for maintenance. Moving her leg to the side, she left herself open to their hot gazes. She licked one finger then slid it the length of her pussy, teasing the clit. An intense wave of pleasure rolled through her. With gentle circles, she played with herself. Not to orgasm but because her masturbation fantasy was playing out right then and there. Boone and Gabby were watching her, stroking their erections beneath the tight fit of their jeans.

She licked her lips and that spurred them to disrobe. They took off their shirts together and sat bare-chested. Big, hard muscles gleamed in the muted light and she bit her bottom lip in an effort not to moan out her appreciation. By this time, she was nice and wet, so she dipped a finger into her pussy, brought it out and licked the digit clean. She tasted slightly sweet, slightly musky. The tease was enough for the men to stand and strip the rest of the way.

Kaiya had seen their cocks before, but now it was daylight and the hard dicks looked even more magnificent. She salivated and fell to her knees, wanting to lick the pre-cum that leaked from the tips. Gabby sat on the bed and directed her attention to his dick, which she eagerly swallowed while Boone moved behind her. He pulled her hips back so she was bent more over Gabby's lap, then he spread her legs apart, grabbed her ass cheeks and proceeded to lick her pussy from behind. She moaned around the thick cock in her mouth, sucking until her cheeks hollowed. The salty taste of Gabby's pre-cum only drove her arousal higher.

Boone made eating pussy an art form. He licked, sucked and fucked her with his tongue. She squirmed, chasing the orgasm that lingered just under the surface. When he slid a finger into her needy channel and hooked his finger up, finding her G-spot, she came instantly. The intense pleasure took over her finer brainpower and she pulled off Gabby's cock. Overcome with the sensations running through her, she cried out her release. Both men let her have the moment, until the climax crashed through her and she slumped. Gabby gathered her hair in one fist and guided her back to his cock. This time, Boone rose behind her and brushed the tip of his penis through her wet slit, sliding up and down. Kaiya arched her hips and, as if he read her mind, he filled her with one thrust.

She gasped around the rod in her mouth. Boone was so large and she was so small that for a brief second, pain filled her as her body adjusted instantly to the tool invading her. He held still, which she appreciated, and when she couldn't stand the pressure anymore, wiggled to get him moving. He pulled out only to slam in again, doing this over and over until ecstasy spiraled through her. Each of his thrusts forced her to take Gabby deep in her throat and she reveled in the fantasy of being a vessel for their lust, being used and fucked like a slut. Gabby tapped her on the shoulder and she looked up at him.

"When I come, don't swallow," he said.

She nodded.

Then he fisted her hair, pulling hard until tears stung her eyes. But she loved it, like a cheap, dirty secret. It only made her lust burn that much hotter. Boone fucked her with force, pumping fast and hard, his cock brushing against a spot that brought a sting of pain mixed with pleasure. He reached around and fingered her clit, and that, combined with his relentless pounding, had her orgasm crashing through her like a thunderbolt. Flames rushed through her body as she burst in a minefield of colors, descending into sated bliss. A moment later, Boone stiffened and pushed into her one more time. The hot jet of his cum filled her, and she wished she could hear any sounds he made.

Gabby fucked her mouth as she watched his face, reveling in the emotions rippling over his features. Suddenly he pulled almost all the way out as thick ropes of spunk landed on her tongue. She was careful to collect every drop, keeping it in her mouth like he'd instructed her to do. When he was done, some ran from the corners of her lips. Gabby opened his eyes, the color hot and molten as he leaned forward and pulled her up for a kiss. He pushed his tongue into her mouth, mindless of the fact that his own cum now coursed across his taste buds. The kiss made the cream run down their faces, but the absolutely kinky act blew her mind and satisfied a deep-seated need. Finally, when the cum was either swallowed or dribbled out, he broke the kiss and stared down into her eyes.

"The dirtier the better," he said.

She smiled. Boone got up and walked into the bathroom, returning a minute later with a wet washcloth. Since it had basically been boarded up the moment Wheels had been taken to the hospital, she wouldn't have to worry about furnishing it right away, which was a plus.

He cleaned her then helped her to stand. She wrapped her arms around him, hugging tightly. Her knees still wobbled a bit from the fantastic sex she'd just had, and she couldn't wait until they could do it again. Kaiya fully embraced her inner nympho, even as she and Gabby headed to the bathroom to gargle and clean their teeth as best as possible.

Chapter Six

While Kaiya took a shower, Gabby rose and grabbed his underwear, mindless of the fact that Boone still lounged naked on the bed. There was no need to be self-conscious about their nudity. They'd served together in the Corp, and Boone made sure he couldn't hurt people at night, which meant he had to tie Gabby up to sleep. That right there screamed a level of intimacy that both, as two heterosexual men, had become very comfortable with.

"Can you do this?" Boone asked.

Gabby finished zipping his jeans before looking at him. They were heading to the store to get some cleaning supplies. "Can I do what?"

"Us and her."

Gabby didn't answer right away. He pulled his ponytail back into the band, smoothing the strands that had become entangled from lovemaking. "I have no problem with us and her."

Boone folded his arms behind his head. "Not what I meant."

Gabby stared steadily at him. "*I* will never share the night with her, but I won't stop you from doing that."

"What about when you start to feel jealous?"

Gabby took a second to reflect on that word. In a normal situation, sure, he'd be jealous as hell. But the way he was forbade him to lead a normal life, not to the mention the fact that this was Boone he was talking to… He shook his head. "I won't allow myself to be jealous."

"Stubborn son of a bitch," Boone muttered.

Gabby looked toward the bathroom door. It stood open, so he could see the outline of Kaiya's beautiful body through the opaque shower door. Hunger twisted his insides, burning through his gut and up into his heart, which beat a little too fast every time he looked at her. From the first moment he'd laid eyes on her, some pull had yanked at him, drawing him closer. He was thirty-eight years old, way too fucking old to be lusting over a much younger woman, and yet he couldn't drag his thoughts from her. Morning, noon and night, she plagued him. Every room he entered in the clubhouse, he constantly searched her out, even knowing she never left her office. He forced himself to stay away, to act nonchalant, even though all he wanted to do was stay by her side and watch over her.

He was pathetic. A man like him didn't deserve someone as lovely as Kaiya. The blood on his hands could never be washed away. Right now, she wanted to live out her fantasies, so he would be that for her. He could fulfill every raunchy, dirty scenario she could dream up, and when it was over, he would walk away knowing she had been the best thing to ever happen to him.

"Gabby—"

"No," he said. He didn't need platitudes, promises or hope. "I've tried to stay away, but I can't. And you know why I can't sleep through the night with her. I can't control the madness."

"You're not mad," Boone whispered.

The shower turned off. Gabby forced himself to stop looking at Kaiya's silhouette to stare Boone in the eyes.

"I've snapped once," he said, his voice dead and cold. "There's no telling when it'll happen again. It's imperative we keep her safe."

Boone sighed and slowly nodded before he rose and reached for his clothes. Gabby left the bedroom, not turning around again. He could never look over his shoulder. Otherwise, he might see all the ghosts ready to drag him to Hell.

* * * *

Sometime later, they walked into the local hardware store together. Gabby held her hand, and Boone followed behind them. She noticed a few stares, but they didn't bother her. People had been staring at her for her entire life, for one reason or another. She was quite proud to be sandwiched between the two handsome specimens.

They strolled through the aisles, stopping at various places. She knew they talked to each another, because the vibrations of their words rumbled back and forth, but she didn't bother trying to see what they said. Gabby picked up a bucket, and Boone became captivated by a display of tools just as she saw a sign for the restroom. She tugged on Gabby's hand and when he turned to her, she signed she had to use it. He gave her a thumbs up, and she finger-waved before heading into the back.

An overhead fluorescent bulb flickered, on the verge of dying, and it cast odd patterns across the floor. As she passed around the corner to where the restrooms were located, a hand grabbed her arm painfully, jerking her to a halt. Her head cracked against the cement blocks when a man pushed her against the wall. Agony sliced through her brain, and she blinked in terror as he waved a gun in her face. It took her a moment to drag her gaze from the deadly weapon to his face, trying to identify him. But she didn't know the stranger hurting her. He was skinny, bald and wore glasses. If anyone had surveyed her on what an attacker would look like, this man would've been the last person she'd ever describe. It took her a moment to realize he was talking to her. She looked at his mouth. Keys? What keys?

"You must have found them by now. I need those keys!"

She shook her head in bewilderment, ignoring the throbbing at the back of her head. Had he mistaken her for someone else? He brought up his fist, as if he meant to backhand her across the face, and her sanity returned. The situation was similar to the one when she'd been kidnapped. Back then, she hadn't known what to do to save herself. But she'd had special training since then, not wanting to once more be the helpless victim who'd been unable to defend herself. Self-defense was not only about knowing the moves but also about being able to push the fear aside to remember the training. The stranger stood directly in front of her, his legs spread. Swiftly, she brought up her knee and hit him right where it counted most. A tortured expression erupted on his face, his eyes rolled back in his head and he doubled over to protect his dick and balls, releasing her. Kaiya didn't waste the opportunity. She shoved him, and just as he fell back like a rag doll, she took off running toward the last place she'd seen Gabby. She rounded the corner and smacked into something hard and unyielding. With a frightened cry, she brought her hands up to defend herself before seeing Boone stare down at her in concern. Gabby was next to him.

She pointed behind her and cried out, not caring the least that her voice was distorted and unattractive. "Help! Man!"

Gabby didn't waste a second. He dropped the bucket he held and dashed the way she'd just run from. He grabbed his gun from the back of his jeans.

"What happened?" Boone signed. He spelled out every word but at least they were able to communicate.

She took a deep breath and signed, "A man grabbed me."

He nodded and took hold of her hand before following after Gabby. He stayed in front of her, protecting her. Their search led outside, where Gabby studied the passing shoppers. His hand was in his jacket pocket so she suspected that's where his gun resided as well.

Gabby and Boone talked, but she couldn't see what they said to each other. Then Gabby turned to her and pulled his hand out of his pocket to sign.

"What happened?"

"A man attacked me. He had a gun."

The two men exchanged furious glances.

"What did he look like?" he asked with his hands.

"Bald. Thin. Glasses."

She read his lips when he said Cipher's name. Bikers did love their gossip, but they knew to keep it in house. Since she could read lips, Kaiya had a knack for learning facts and some of those facts had been about what Romeo had done to the old accountant. The man was supposed to be banished from the state, so why would he come back to the one place he knew could be a death sentence if he was caught?

She tugged on Gabby's arm. His eyes were wild, angry, and for a moment, she saw the fierce soldier inside him. "I think I should go to my office."

"Why your office?"

"If that was Cipher, I need to know why he came back for keys," she signed.

"What do you mean keys?"

"He demanded a set of keys. Said I must have found them. They've got to be in the office since it was his too."

"Slow down," Gabby said. "You're signing too fast again. Now, he wanted to keys to what?"

She shrugged. She may not know the answer to that but she was determined to find out.

Gabby glanced over her head and related to Boone what she'd demanded. Boone narrowed his stormy gray eyes.

"You take her back to the compound," he ordered. "I'm going to try to find that fucker."

Gabby nodded and took her hand. He led her away from the hardware store toward his bike. Seconds later, they raced out of the parking lot. As they zoomed in the direction of the clubhouse, she couldn't help but wonder how Cipher had known she was at the hardware store—unless he'd been watching her. A rumble of unease skittered through her at the disturbing thought.

* * * *

Anger burned hotly through Boone. He hoped like fuck to find the asshole so he had an excuse to punch the ever-living shit out of someone. He rode up and down the street, looking for Cipher, determined to finish what Romeo had started. The little shit dared lay a hand on his woman, threaten her, *hurt* her… The son of a bitch deserved to die.

He went through the old warehouse district, the closed-down area with busted-out windows and graffiti painted everywhere. The Shanks had once used this section for their own personal playground, getting stoned and shooting the glass. Now that they were gone, it seemed like a good hideout for an ex-Brother to hide. Only the place had a ghost town atmosphere about the area as the wind whistled through the hollowed buildings. His instinct told him Cipher wasn't there, so he throttled away, toward the hardware store. He kept glancing around, hoping he'd find the little prick, but there wasn't any sign of the bald-headed accountant.

As he headed back to the compound, he couldn't stop thinking about Kaiya. What the hell had sucker-punched him until all he thought about was her? Was she a damn witch who had put a spell on him? Because ever since he had taken a lick of her cream, he'd been addicted. Even riding his bike was difficult, although that was one adjective he didn't need to think about right then as he rolled through a turn. His fucking dick was like concrete. It always was when he thought about Kaiya.

He had no idea where the three of them were headed. Hell, he hadn't even thought about a relationship in years. Ever since he and Gabby had gotten out of the Marines, he'd been focused on the club and making sure his best friend didn't succumb to the demons howling and clawing inside him. Boone refused to let his best friend become just another suicide statistic, and if that meant tying his ass up every night so he wouldn't hurt himself, then so be it. Of course, Gabby had been acting completely different ever since Kaiya had shown up in their lives, and for that, Boone would be forever grateful. The man might think he had to be emotionless and deny his feelings, but Boone knew it was just a matter of time before Gabby could no longer hide what he felt.

Boone may not know where this relationship was heading, or what the conclusion of it might be, but what he did know was that he needed to protect Kaiya and it burned through his gut. If he got his hands on Cipher, the motherfucker would take his last tortured breath staring into the eyes of the man who had finally brought him down. That Boone vowed to himself.

* * * *

Kaiya didn't bother to linger in the clubhouse. She burst into her office and ignored the throbbing through her head. Standing in the doorway, she tried to look at the office through new eyes. Where would Cipher have hidden a set of keys? She'd cleaned the place from top to bottom, had gone over it with a fine-toothed comb. Of course, she hadn't been looking for keys when she'd sorted the trash from the valuables. Something that small could be anywhere.

Why were they so valuable to Cipher? What lock did they open? There wasn't much in the room, just a desk, a chair, a trashcan, a paper shredder and a bookcase stuffed full of binders, books and papers. All of it cheap furniture she could've bought at Wal-Mart. Going with instinct, she went to the desk and sat in the chair. She had already sorted through the drawers, but gave them another search just in case. Nothing. Was it just a misunderstanding? Perhaps the man wasn't Cipher and had her mixed up with someone else. Maybe the keys meant nothing. She went to slam the top drawer shut and felt the wood resist a little as it slid in. It was very subtle, and she hadn't given it much thought before, but now she wondered if the slight drag was from something else.

Kneeling, she pulled the drawer out and set it on top of the desk before sliding her arm inside the dark, narrow passage. At first, all she encountered were the tracks that guided the bottom of the drawer. Then her fingertips brushed against something, and she grabbed it before yanking it out. It was a small envelope, and when she opened it, three dull brass keys fell into her palm. She blinked at them, unsure if she was really seeing them. They were short with a wide base and plastic covered their ends. A set of uniform numbers were etched into the metal. Kaiya knew they weren't house keys so she sat in her chair, replaced the drawer and fired up her laptop.

Searching for the identification of the three keys was flat out tedious, and it didn't help her headache at all. One key pretty much resembled the next one. Plus she had no idea what she was looking for in the first place, let alone what they could possibly be for. After a while, the dull ache from where her head had slapped against the wall flared from the intensity of staring at the laptop screen. She rubbed her temples, wanting to give up. Without any direction, it was like trying to find a needle in a haystack.

As she stretched her cramped muscles, she ran her gaze over the new photos on the Internet web search and landed on a photo of a man holding a set of keys in his hand. They looked strikingly similar to the ones on her desk that it suddenly dawned on her what the keys were and she hurried to open up a new website for bus terminals.

Half an hour later, she made her way to Romeo's office. Boone sat in one seat facing the president of the club and, when she knocked, they both turned to see her. She held up a sign that said, "I need to inform you of something."

Romeo nodded and said to Boone, "Go get Gabby and Dax."

Boone gave her a concerned, searching glance before leaving her with Romeo. They had been working closely together for a few weeks and she'd come to know him as funny and caring, but fuck with him and he gave no quarter. He seemed like a fair man, an honorable one to his men, his club and to Chloe. Yet she had no illusions that the switchblade he carried wasn't strictly for decoration.

It didn't take long for Boone to collect Gabby and Dax, and the office suddenly seemed too small with all the large male bodies present. When Romeo nodded to her, she held up another handwritten sign that asked, "Did Boone and Gabby tell you about the man who attacked me earlier?"

Romeo nodded.

She laid down the piece of paper. That had been her last sign. She signed to him, angling so that Gabby could read and translate. "I think I know why Cipher came back."

That had everyone's attentions. Romeo shared a quick look with Dax.

"Go on," Boone said.

"Cipher invented his own shorthand, and although I'll probably never be able to understand it completely, I did manage to figure out his money trail."

She waited until Gabby told them what she'd said.

"Money trail?" Romeo asked.

"He made two ledgers," she continued. "You weren't the only ones he stole from."

Almost immediately after Gabby related what she said, rage darkened Romeo's handsome features. He leaned forward in his chair and pinned her with an angry stare. She was very glad she wasn't the object of his wrath.

"Are you saying he not only fleeced the club, but swindled Shepard as well?" Romeo asked, in what she assumed would be a stone-cold voice.

She nodded.

"So where's the extra money?"

She laid out the three keys on the table. "In three separate locations."

All the men stared at her in shock.

Boone tapped her on the shoulder, and she glanced at him.

"Do you know where these locations are?"

She pointed to the first key. "This is a key for the lockers in the Greyhound terminal in Lincoln." She pushed the second one forward. "This is for the lockers in the Greyhound terminal in Omaha. And the third? It's located in Sioux City, South Dakota."

Romeo folded his arms and leaned back in his chair. She could feel the tension and rage boiling just under the surface. "Up Interstate Twenty-Nine."

"Cipher went on that last meth run with me to Sioux City," Dax said. "Right before Shepard's double life was exposed and I missed all the fun."

"I wish I had killed that fucker now." Kaiya read Romeo's lips.

"Well, we have the keys and we know where they money is," Boone said. "Gabby and I planned on heading to Canada to meet with Red Eye. We can stop at each place and just pick it up."

Kaiya banged on the table to grab their attention. "I want to go," she signed. "I need to see how much is there and measure it against his books. Perhaps I can figure out the rest of his shorthand if I have a monetary comparison to look for."

She watched Romeo's face as Gabby related her request.

Romeo studied her, then he glanced at Gabby. "Are you going to be able to handle that?"

For a split second, a petrified look crossed through his eyes. If she wasn't so in tune to watching people, she probably would have missed it. But there was no denying the thought of spending time with her terrified him, and the idea stabbed into her heart.

"Yes," Gabby said.

She knew he lied and it pissed her off.

Slowly, Romeo nodded. "Very well." He met her gaze. "This time, Kaiya. All right? Shit, Chloe's going to skin me for allowing this."

Irritation at Gabby's fear spiked through her. It also irked her that Romeo had to approve of her going, that he thought he ruled her. She was free, damn it. Romeo Barrigan would not replace her grandfather's autocratic rule with his own. Rubbing her forehead, she gathered the three keys and marched away, head down.

Back in her office, she took a deep breath to calm the anger trembling through her body. A hand on her arm made her flinch and she spun, her fists ready to defend herself. Gabby stood there, watching her with narrowed eyes. He held a can of soda and two white pills.

"Aspirin," he said.

She grudgingly accepted them, placed them on her tongue and washed them down with the cold drink. The closing of the door caught her attention, and she glanced up at Gabby questioningly. His eyes glittered in the low light.

"Why did you not like what Romeo said?" he signed.

She smacked her hand down on the desk. She might not have been able to hear the bang, but the pain radiating up her arm made her feel a tad better.

"Romeo wasn't the only one who made me angry," she signed. "*You* didn't like the thought of me being around."

"Not the way you think," he said. "I suffer from PTSD. I don't want to accidentally hurt you."

Okay, that somewhat eased the ache that had been building in her chest. Still, she stuck her chin up in defiance.

"That first day, I told you I'm free." There. That was short and precise. No way could he misunderstand that. "I won't live under anyone's thumb again. You, Romeo, Boone, none of you can tell me what to do!"

"What he said was for the good of the club."

"I am club!"

He shook his head. "No, you're family. Outside the club, Chloe is Romeo's number one concern and he knows she's not going to like having you away from her."

She hated that what he said made sense. "It sounded like a reluctant excuse."

He cupped her face with one hand and rubbed his thumb over her lips. "You're being bratty."

Her mouth fell open, and annoyance flared once again. *Bratty?* Who did he think he was? Gabby knew nothing about being a prisoner—stuck behind high walls, unable to communicate with the outside world.

Slowly dying, day by day as the life was sucked out in minute increments. She reached out and hit him on the chest with a fist. Lightning fast, he spun her around until her back pressed against his front. He held her locked within the circle of his arms, and although she wiggled and fought, he kept a firm grip. It was like trying to break free of iron shackles, and soon she panted from the exertion of going nowhere. He loosened his hold only long enough to turn her so she could read his lips.

"Bratty girls get spanked," he said.

Although it was supposed to be a threat, she went from pissed-off to aroused in a nano-second. Gabby didn't give her much time to think about the implication of his words because in the next second, he sat in her own chair and had her bent over. He wrapped one leg around hers, locking her in place, while he caressed one big beefy hand over her ass cheeks. Kaiya struggled, although it was half-hearted at best. No way could he possibly mean to *spank* her. She'd always imagined spanking came with sexual play, not actually used for punishment. And yet he pulled his hand away then brought it down a second later, smacking her hard across one butt cheek. Not censoring her voice, she cried out. Again, he spanked her and again, she yelled, beyond pissed. Yet with each crack of his hand, the pain was sharp, brief and began to migrate straight to her clit. She'd forgotten to count but it wasn't long before she calmed to actually look forward to the next, drifting in a sort of euphoric haze. In fact, she didn't even protest when he stopped and draped her over her desk. All she knew was that her pussy was dripping, her ass was on fire, and a sense of peace had segued through her brain.

Slowly, Gabby stripped her of her pants, followed by her panties, and still she simply lay on the desk, trying to gather her scattered wits. He sat in the chair and ran his hands up and down her thighs, settling on her still-smarting cheeks. He separated them and cool air rushed over her anus, causing her to shudder and rouse her a little more from her stupor. He ran his tongue over her rosette and a new thrill shot through her languid body. Gabby eased the tip up and down the puckered flesh then dipped into her heated channel. Kaiya had already been creaming her panties from the spanking, but the stimulation against the nerve endings had the juices flowing like a sieve. And when he reached around her hips to find her clit, it was too much to bear and she convulsed with a spine-tingling orgasm.

Gabby caressed her through her climax until tiny little shivers rolled through her, then he pulled away. She vaguely heard the zipper go down on his jeans but there was no confusing when he nudged her legs open farther and settled between her splayed thighs. He brushed his cock teasingly through her slit, and she wiggled her hips impatiently. With a mighty shove, he plunged into her. Kaiya emitted a tiny shriek as his cock buried into her, the force sending her forward on the desk. He held still for a moment, letting her adjust to his length and girth. He was big, like Boone, but she was so wet that the discomfort immediately melted away.

Gabby pumped in shallow little thrusts at first, but quickly gave way to something deeper and harder. She wished she could hear the sounds, especially all the noises from him, and once again, she cursed her deafness. In and out, he pushed, gaining in speed until he was pounding her pussy like a madman. Then out of nowhere, he slapped her ass. Not as hard as the punishment had been, but still, her already sensitive cheek lit up like a live wire had touched it. She yelped and bucked, but rubbed his fingers over her swollen clit, calming her. He tortured her like this over and over. First a spank then a rub, spiraling her higher and higher until the dam burst. Kaiya cried out as her orgasm took over, her whole body shaking as he fucked her with all ten inches crammed into her tight pussy.

With one last thrust, Gabby erupted deep within her cunt. Shot after shot of hot cum bathed her, filling her until he collapsed forward over her back, holding her hips. The man had stamina, ejaculating the last bit of his cum deep into her as he kissed the back of her neck. Her heart beat frantically as she gulped in air. Finally, Gabby pulled from her, his cock slipping out of her body. Fluid gushed down her thighs but she was too sated to do much about it. Gabby knelt behind her and began cleaning her with a cloth and when she looked, she saw it was his T-shirt. His bare chest gleamed with sweat, making his tats stand out against his tanned skin. Excitement flared to life even though her body still quivered from the amazing orgasms he'd given her.

Gabby smiled and winked, and she had to wonder if she shouldn't be bratty more often.

Chapter Seven

The dimness of the dingy and depressing bar encompassed him, matching his attitude to a tee. Cipher stared into the amber glass of his beer bottle as if he could glean all of life's mysteries from its bottomless depths. Desperation made his stomach roll sickeningly. The warm beer did not help the matter at all.

"That was a bold move you made today."

He looked at the man sitting next to him—tall, big, mean looking. The blackness of his eyes held a dark, soulless reflection, and a shiver raced across Cipher's skin. He knew, without a doubt, that evil lived inside this man.

"I was watching them, which means I've been watching you." The man gave a chuckle devoid of amusement. "You must have titanium balls sitting out in the open where any of those fuckers can find you."

"Leave me the fuck alone," Cipher muttered. The guy was giving him the creeps.

"You know, I thought Boone and that big silent guy were lovers."

That caught his attention. "You mean Gabby?"

"That his name?" The man pulled a cigarette out of a pack and lit it with a silver lighter. He took a long drag before exhaling the smoke. It encircled his head like a misty halo. "And then this little Jap girl comes along and suddenly both men are fucking her. What got you so fired up that you attacked their woman?"

Cipher shook his head. "Who in the hell are you?"

The man took another deep hit before grinding the cigarette out. "The name's Vicious. From your actions today, I believe we have a mutual enemy."

No way in hell did Cipher want to talk to the man, but anger stirred deep inside his core. The bitter taste of hatred burned the back of his throat. "You mean the Men of Hell?"

"I meant their fucking V.P. Boone Tempest."

Just hearing the man's name had him squeezing his hand into a fist, ready to let his anger fly. Boone had been the one to stuff a bandana in his mouth when his cries of being tortured had become too loud. He really wished the asshole were in front of him so he could punch the ever-living shit out of the man.

"Why'd you go after the bitch?" Vicious asked again.

Maybe it was the need to expunge the fury that ate at him like cancer. Maybe it was the fact that Vicious' deadly eyes offered retribution. Suddenly, he wanted to do everything possible to hurt the men who had hurt him. He turned toward Vicious. "There are three lockers with money in them and *she* has the keys. I *really* need my property back."

Vicious turned eerily still, as if his skin had turned to marble. His face held a blank expression and Cipher had the uneasy feeling that the man was staring into his soul, devouring it slowly.

"I think we can help each other," Vicious said calmly.

"All I want is my goddamn money," Cipher muttered.

"Really? That's all you want?"

And before Cipher knew what was happening, Vicious slapped him on the back, directly on his right shoulder blade. It had been almost two months since Romeo had sliced his tattoo off and he was still healing from the fucking skinning. Regrowing skin took a long fucking time. Agony ripped through him and he couldn't stop the cry that escaped his mouth.

Vicious frowned and stood to pull back the leather jacket Cipher wore. If he weren't in such fucking pain, he'd push the asshole away, but as it was, he was trying his damnedest not to pass out.

"What the fuck?" Vicious asked. "You're bleeding."

"They took my tat."

Vicious let him go and sat back down. Cipher downed the rest of his beer, not caring in the least that it was room temperature. He desperately needed alcohol now to dull the fire licking through his wound.

"They fucking made you bleed?" Vicious asked. "Don't you want to hurt them the same way? Slice off a piece of them where it hurts most?"

All his simmering resentment suddenly burst forward, and Cipher pounded his fist on the scarred bar top. "I want to fucking rip them apart."

Vicious' mouth curled into a satisfied smirk, the thin veneer of civility ripped away. Malice glinted in his dark eyes, and Cipher was surprised acid didn't drip from the canines peeking from beneath his lips.

"So we'll start with Boone. And get your fucking money."

* * * *

As Kaiya suspected, Chloe was all over the place, signing with angry points and jabs. When the words rambled together, Kaiya simply read her lips. Chloe could rival a soldier's vocabulary when having a very bad day.

"This is fucking stupid!" she ranted. "Most fucking insane thing I've ever heard of. Of course you can't go on a fucking bike ride to Canada. That's like...millions of miles away. You'll get hurt. You'll fall off. You'll break your ass!"

"I'm not going to break my ass," Kaiya signed back. "And it's only six hundred miles. The circumference of the Earth is less than twenty-five thousand miles. To go millions of miles I'd have to get a rocket ship—"

Chloe waved her hands in agitation. "So *not* the fucking point!"

Kaiya turned her head to hide her smile. Chloe continued her curse-word-laden tirade while Boone and Gabby watched her impassively with their arms folded across their chests. Kaiya gave them apologetic glances, but they just shrugged. Obviously, they were aware of how Chloe could work herself up. Finally, out of desperation, she grabbed hold of her cousin's head and brought their foreheads together. Chloe covered her hands and they stood like that for a long time, until their breathing synchronized and her cousin had calmed. It was an old trick she used to do whenever her outbursts got a little too wild. Chloe wasn't a bad person, but her past had definitely messed her up.

"I'm going to be fine," she whispered in Chloe's ear. At least, she hoped it was a whisper. It was difficult to remember what the volume was for a whisper. When Chloe didn't pull away or cringe at the sharp pitch, Kaiya relaxed.

Chloe nodded, not answering. She didn't need to. Kaiya knew her cousin well. She might have a temper and might act before thinking, but she loved with her whole heart, and when something moved out of her control, she lashed out. Throughout her stay in the psychiatric hospitals, only Kaiya had been able to calm her.

They stayed like that for some time, until Chloe pulled back to stare her into her eyes. A small, sad smile lingered on her lips.

"When did you grow up?" Chloe asked.

Kaiya snorted and dropped her hands to step back. "I'm only four years younger than you."

"So?" Chloe signed. "You're still a baby."

"I'm a woman. And these two big men are mine. Okay?"

Chloe rolled her eyes but nodded. Blowing her a kiss, Kaiya headed over to her men. She wore jeans and a button-down. A far cry from the silk she'd worn the first time she rode a bike, but even slipping on the leather jacket and helmet Boone and Gabby had provided her, she had a funny feeling she still looked out of place. She gave herself a mental shrug. Didn't really matter. Going on this run with her two men meant a lot because it represented a step toward being truly free.

Chloe walked up to them, put her hands on her hips and narrowed her eyes. "You hurt her in any way, shape or form, and I will personally dissect your balls. You know I can do it. Without anesthesia. Maybe just a paralytic so you can feel your scrotum being cut in half."

Kaiya didn't hear what they said, but after that vivid description, she was sure it was promise after promise of them being on their best behavior. Chloe pursed her lips and folded her arms, but her cousin didn't protest anymore.

She would be taking turns sitting behind each man, but the first part of the journey to Lincoln she mounted the bike behind Boone. Wrapping her arms around him, excitement gripped her. As she gave a wave to Chloe, she couldn't help the silly grin plastered on her face.

Chapter Eight

They arrived in Lincoln almost three hours later, and by then Kaiya couldn't feel her ass or her legs, and her hands were a little shaky. As she dismounted, Boone held onto her while Gabby registered them at the small motel they'd stopped at. It was the kind of place where all the units were ground level, extending on either side from the office, and the cleanliness factor was definitely suspect.

"It won't have bugs, will it?" she signed tentatively.

Boone shook his head. "Nah. The Men of Hell own this place. It may not look like much on the outside, but it's clean and comfortable."

That startled her. "I don't remember seeing revenue from a motel on the books."

"It's owned by the mother chapter, not the Bair one. There are a whole slew of places like this throughout Nebraska."

Gabby strode back to them and held out a key to her. Kaiya accepted it, confused when he kept another one for himself. She still didn't understand why he wouldn't stay the night with her. Did it mean Boone wouldn't sleep with her either? Their rooms were located on the end, right next to each other with a connecting door between them, which gave her a small dose of consolation. Perhaps each man just wanted his space. Perhaps...she was just a convenient fuck.

That hurt—a lot. Even though she was pragmatic and knew they were simply having some fun, she was afraid her heart had already begun a decent into something deeper. She went to her room, and the men went to theirs. She sighed, wondering if this was how it was always going to be—with a door dividing them. Being on a bike didn't allow for a suitcase so she could only bring necessities in a backpack, which meant there wasn't much to unpack. Moments later, a knock came from the divider, and she opened the door to reveal Boone holding up his phone. He had taken off his Men of Hell jacket and stood in a plain black T-shirt and black jeans. Thinking about what those jeans contained made her salivate for a lick.

"I just ordered a pizza," he said.

She read his lips and nodded, forcing her mind out of the gutter.

He gestured for her to follow him into a room identical to hers, down to the same ugly comforter on each of the beds. Gabby lay on the one farthest from their connecting door, looking utterly relaxed with his ankles crossed and an arm was thrown over his eyes.

"Is he okay?" she signed to Boone.

Boone nodded. "Tired," he signed back.

He turned on the television, and a news channel came up. She was able to follow along while the anchor presented the facts, but once it cut away to a featured story, she was lost. Boone, however, threw the remote on the bed and pulled her into his arms. She rested her head on his chest, wishing she could hear his heart thumping, but settling for feeling the vibration pound through his torso. They stayed like that for a while, until he pulled back to answer the knock she hadn't heard. She watched him pay for the large pizza and a two-liter soda before shutting and locking the door. He set the food on the circular table, called out to Gabby and gestured for her to sit. Gabby joined them and they dug into the big, gooey pizza.

She ate, not bothering to pay attention to the two men. Her life had consisted of solitary meals, starting back when her parents had been too scared to do anything else in case they hurt her. They would've wrapped her up in a bubble room if they'd had their way. When they died in a car accident, she had thought she'd live with her aunt and uncle, Chloe's parents, until she learned how volatile that situation had been. Her grandfather had taken over raising her, and she'd had a bevy of servants to meet her every need, including her schooling. Numbers had always been easy to her, so she'd gravitated toward being an accountant with the thought of working in her grandfather's business someday.

That dream had been nixed the day she'd been kidnapped. When she'd returned to her grandfather's side, he had sent her to Japan where she'd had to learn sign language all over again. Japanese sign language was different from its American counterpart, derived from the complex *kanji* writing system as well as finger spelling. Life hadn't been exactly fair to her, but she'd never moaned or complained because her grandfather had been confused about what to do with her. He'd done his best to raise her within the confines of what he knew. But now, having tasted the freedom of doing what she wanted, of potentially having a permanent home without safety walls, was a high she never wanted to end. Now she knew exactly how addicts felt.

Gabby tapped her hand. Startled, she dragged her mind away from the past and glanced at him. While she'd eaten only a slice, they'd managed to demolish the rest of the pizza.

"We're going to the locker," Gabby signed. "You stay here."

It took her a moment to process the fact that she wasn't included. "No. I want to come with you to the bus terminal."

"It's too dangerous," Boone said.

Once again, someone was deciding what was best for her. Anger lanced through her, and she rose so abruptly that her chair tilted a little. "You do *not* get to decide what's too dangerous for me!"

"Sit," Gabby ordered.

She shook her head mutinously. "Do not tell me what to do."

"Then don't act like a child!" Gabby signed.

By the set slash of his mouth and the darkening of his eyes, it was obvious that he was pissed. Why, she hadn't a clue, but Kaiya also didn't care that he didn't like her attitude. She wasn't their prisoner. She could make her own decisions.

"I discovered those keys. I should be the one to find out what's in the locker," she signed.

Boone and Gabby shared a quick look. She braced for what they were going to say next.

"Cipher's attack on you was desperate," Boone said.

She nodded, agreeing with that statement. "If he was willing to go after you, knowing Gabby and I were only steps away, he'll have no compunction about doing something worse in order to save whatever is in that locker."

She *knew* he made sense. She was a liability because she wouldn't be able to hear if there was an attack of some kind, but to be causally dismissed, like every other time in her life, irked her fiercely. Especially from these two men who knew her intimately. She wanted to be their woman, not someone they only tolerated in the bedroom.

"I won't get in the way," she signed, pressing her argument.

Boone ran a hand over his face. He was vice president of the club, and though Gabby had a mind of his own, he wouldn't act against Boone's decision. Kaiya understood the hierarchy between them. They were friends, but they were Brothers in the club first, and just like her grandfather's organization, friendship took a backseat to commands.

"How about this," Boone said. He did a mixture of talking and signing with what he understood. "If nothing happens this time around, you can go with us when we hit the locker in Omaha."

She lifted up her hands to reply then lowered them again to think. They were willing to compromise. He wasn't forcing her to back down. She appreciated the fact that he wasn't dismissing her once more. Slowly, she nodded.

Boone smiled and stood. He leaned over the table and kissed her quickly on the mouth. Then he turned to head over to his bed where his saddlebag rested. He opened it and pulled out two guns then ejected the clips to inspect them before reloading and chambering a round in each one. He flipped on the safety. Although he wore a gun holster at his waist, he pulled out a double shoulder harness and proceeded to gear up.

Gabby stood, capturing her attention. They expected trouble. The grim countenance on his face reflected all his wayward emotions a split second before shutting down and wiping them away. But in that moment, she'd seen enough to be very worried for her men. It almost made her glad she hadn't insisted on going with them, just to give him some peace of mind.

He held out his hand to her and she placed her much smaller one in it, admiring the contrast between his skin and hers. She liked both guys, and loved how they excited her. Gabby seemed to be the strength while Boone was the sturdy rock anchoring him. She may not know all their dynamics, but she appreciated that they didn't have jealousy between them.

"We'll be back soon," Gabby said.

She nodded.

He bent his head, kissing her, and slid his tongue across the seam of her lips. She opened for him. Gabby plunged inside, stealing her breath as her body came alive for his touch. He tasted of garlic and cheese and she wished they would lay her on the bed so he could fuck her. He pulled away all too soon and walked over to get ready as well. When they were done, they looked like they were ready for war.

They talked to one another, and Kaiya wrapped her arms around herself. From the one-sided conversation she read from Boone's lips, they really expected Cipher to show up, guns blazing. It made her pause. What if something *did* happen? She had no doubt that Boone and Gabby could protect themselves, but a desperate man was unpredictable, and shit happened. She hurried over to them and threw her arms around them at the same time—squeezing as hard as she could. Although she had quite a bit of height for a woman, they still towered over her a good five inches. They hugged her back, then they were gone, striding out the door. It shut behind them, and suddenly the room pulsed hauntingly around her. Alone and lonely, she hugged herself tightly, and sat on the edge of the bed.

* * * *

"She's prickly about being left out, huh?" Boone asked.

"No. She's prickly about being told what to do. She was in a hell of a frame of mind after Romeo's decision."

"One you took care of, I take it."

Gabby smirked. "She was a bad girl who needed spanking."

Boone smiled and straddled his bike. He put on his helmet, waited until Gabby gave him a nod that he was ready, then they roared out of the parking lot. The late afternoon shadows crept across the road, and the sun blazed directly in their driving path. It was cool despite the fact that it was July, but his heavy jacket kept him from being cold. It also concealed the two weapons strapped to his side as well as a third gun at his waist. Going to the locker made him and Gabby targets, giving Cipher the element of surprise. The asshole might have been the accountant of the Men of Hell, but he knew how to use a gun and he was still out there.

They pulled into the bus terminal, which wasn't really a bus station, only a narrow building that hosted the buses coming and going. As he turned off the rumbling engine and dismounted, many people gawked at them. Boone figured he and Gabby looked a little out of place among the crowd with suitcases and family members. He wasn't the least bit interested in the convenience store and walked around to the back, where two rows of storage lockers waited under an awning. The key had a large number sixteen on it so

Gabby took point and watched the surrounding area while Boone located the locker and inserted the key into the small locker to open it. Inside lay a small duffel bag. He pulled it out and let the locker shut. Opening the bag, he glimpsed a bundle of cash and swore under his breath. Yes, he had suspected he'd find money, but now that it confirmed just how much Cipher had backstabbed them, his blood burned even hotter for payback.

"What is it?" Gabby asked.

"What we thought," he replied. "I was willing to give Cipher the benefit of doubt, but this fucking shit just pisses me off."

Gabby nodded.

"Come on, let's get out of here. No need to press our luck."

He led the way back to the bikes, gripping the duffel bag tightly. The money belonged to the Men of Hell. Even though Chloe had helped them out, he knew Romeo wanted to pay her back. Whatever cash was in here would help restore their coffers so they could be independent again.

By the time they hit the road to go back to Kaiya, twilight had fallen. The bus depot had been located in the middle of nowhere, in an industrial section of the city with little more than trees and warehouses around. Boone just started to relax when a vehicle jumped out at them from a dark service area, breaks squealing as the car's back end whipped around. If Boone hadn't been so experienced on his bike, or known his machine by heart, the car might have banged into him. But Boone swerved and accelerated, peeling away so rapidly that the bike shuddered under him, protesting the sudden sideways dancing forced upon it. Gabby throttled up next to him and the car gave chase. He pulled a gun free from his holster, flipped the safety off with his thumb and fired at the piece-of-shit jalopy. Beside him, Gabby did the same. Two sets of guns fired back, one from the driver's side and one from the passenger. Bullets whipped by his head, and he ducked, returning fire. Just as his gun clicked empty, a loud pop boomed from the motor, and the vehicle swerved into the ditch as steam erupted from the engine. He and Gabby accelerated down the road, but quickly slowed enough to turn around and head back to the ruined car. He slipped the empty gun back into its holster and grabbed his other one as they approached the dead vehicle.

"Son of a bitch!" Gabby snarled as they came to a halt.

The doors stood wide open and no one was around. Whoever had been in the car had fled.

"Cipher," Boone said grimly. "And he wasn't working alone."

"Fucking cowards for running."

Boone looked around the empty road. Their car chase had gone unnoticed. However, he had the distinct feeling they were being watched. "Maybe they ran for a reason."

Gabby stared into the dark tree line. "Luring us?"

"Not sure." Boone put his gun back. "Let's get the hell out of here, only let's split up and circle the long way back to the motel."

Gabby nodded, and they zoomed away, leaving the accident far behind.

Chapter Nine

"We could've killed them!" Cipher raged. "Why didn't you let me shoot?"

Vicious grabbed his T-shirt and twisted, bringing Cipher face to face with him. Madness swam in his eyes, and it scared Cipher to his core.

"Because that's too easy. Boone has to suffer. He *needs* to bleed out every drop of blood in his heart and I *must* watch him die emotionally before I finally slit his throat."

Cipher blinked and once again he wondered what in the hell he'd been thinking to make this devil his ally. "Why do you hate him so much?"

Vicious released him and stepped back. The madness had been replaced with a stone-cold killer he'd come to know. The man who had owned the old car they'd used to shoot at Gabby and Boone resided in the trunk with a bullet in his brain. A shiver of unease crept down Cipher's back. He'd best be careful or he'd end up with a similar fate.

"Doesn't matter why," Vicious replied. "What matters is that we know they're going after your merchandise. We know where they're heading."

"The third locker is the most important," Cipher said, darting his gaze around on the dirty little shithole they'd rented. Or more specifically, one that *he* had rented. Vicious said he didn't have any cash. Typical. Cipher watched a roach scurry up the cigarette-smoke-stained wall and he couldn't help but think that the bug was symbolic. He really needed to get away from this crazy asshole. "More than just the money is in it."

Vicious cocked his head. "Like what?"

"A journal. I need it."

"A fucking book?" Vicious shook his head. "You people with degrees are really fucked up, you know that?"

Cipher hesitated for a second before plunging on with his counter offer. There was only way to assure that he stayed alive when this partnership dissolved. "I'll give you all of the cash. All I want is that journal."

"You're talking about three hundred grand?"

Cipher nodded. "Plus you get Boone and Gabby."

"All for a book? What the fuck's in there?"

Every muscle in Cipher's body tensed. There'd be no rest for him tonight since he would now have to keep one eye open on this crazy motherfucker. "Nothing that would interest you."

Vicious narrowed his eyes and rubbed his chin. "That's a good pay off."

"It is."

"All right," Vicious replied softly. "You've got a deal. Though I'm coming out the winner in this negotiation."

Cipher didn't dispute that. He needed to let the other man think that.

"Then we skip Omaha and go right to Sioux City," Vicious said. "Wait. What about the money in Omaha?"

"They'll be expecting us. Let them collect the duffel bag and come to us. It'll confuse them when we don't show up." Vicious flashed a bone-chilling smile. "I have big plans for Sioux City, and once we kill them, you'll have all you deserve."

Cipher didn't like the way he phrased that. "You mean my journal, correct?"

Vicious gave one, slow nod. "Of course."

"Why can't we just pry open the locker door?"

"Now what fun would that be? No, Gabby and Boone require something…explosive. Something they'll never see coming. Ambush them when they're vulnerable, when they think they're safe. Then proceed to kill Gabby slowly so Boone knows what it's like to lose someone he loves."

"Is that what he did to you?" Cipher asked. "Kill someone you love?"

For a second, Vicious' gaze turned inward, as if he were remembering something—or someone. Then his veneer cracked just a bit and bitter love shone through, until reality turned and hatred once more replaced any type of softer emotion.

"Boone's going to wish he'd never been born," Vicious said firmly. The promise was unmistakable.

* * * *

Kaiya paced back and forth, not because she was scared for Boone and Gabby, but because she was very impatient to see what the locker held. Odds were it was probably the money Cipher had fleeced. She'd done the books, knew how good he had been at hiding the transactions, but how much had he taken? With the exact amount, it would be a helluva lot easier to decode Cipher's shorthand.

The distant reverberation of a motorcycle filtered through the room and she peeked out the window, expecting to see both Harleys pull up in front of the motel room. But the bike circled around back, and she waited for a moment before she went back to pacing. Questions slammed into her head as worry settled in her chest. She hadn't missed the fact that only Boone had returned. A few moments later, he entered the room holding a duffel bag that he tossed on the bed. He closed the door quickly behind him, then he turned off the light. He slid her a grim look as he moved to the window. He pushed the curtain aside only wide enough to peek out of the side. Unease slithered down Kaiya's back.

She tugged on Boone's arm and when he looked at her, she signed her questions. "What's wrong? Where's Gabby?"

"We were shot at," he said. "I think they wanted to tail us."

He resumed looking out the window. It didn't escape her notice that he hadn't answered her second question. A few minutes later, he went to the door and opened it. Gabby walked in, then they locked the door tightly.

Kaiya's heart thundered, and she quickly ran to him and threw her arms around him. He hugged her back, but that wasn't what she wanted. She shoved him far enough away to run her hands over him, then she switch to Boone and did the same thing to him. She wanted to make sure they weren't hurt.

"We're fine," Gabby signed, understanding her actions.

After a few more minutes of looking out the window, Boone relaxed enough to leave his surveillance. He turned on the nightstand light before reaching for the duffel bag. He unzipped it and flipped it over. Ten stacks of one hundred dollar bills, each labeled with a band denoting the amount as ten thousand, tumbled onto the bed. Kaiya's mouth fell open. She had expected money, but if this locker had a hundred thousand dollars and there were two more keys, then Cipher had been a very busy accountant.

"I thought there'd be more," Gabby signed.

She stared at him in surprise. "More?"

He shrugged. "I thought Cipher would've been greedier."

"Skimming money takes a deft sleight of hand." She gestured to the cash on the bed. "From what I've learned of Shepard, he wasn't too trusting. He was probably studying those books too."

"That's club money," Boone said.

She nodded and scooped up the ten stacks to set them on the table. Kaiya hurried through to her own room and grabbed her laptop. She had to sacrifice clothing to bring this along, but she needed her accounting program to plug in the new variables to Cipher's little code. She had no idea what she would discover, or if his code meant anything at all, but her gut told her that Cipher wouldn't go to all this trouble for a simple Dear Diary.

Sometime later, a hand touched her shoulder and she looked up. Gabby stood at her side. "You've been at this for an hour."

Surprised, she looked at her computer and saw that he was correct. She straightened, her cramped muscles protesting the sudden stretching.

"I'm sorry," she signed. "I didn't realize how late it was."

He held out his hand to her. "Come. It's time you relaxed."

"He's hiding something. I know it."

"I believe you," he said. "But you need a break."

The unmistakable bulge of his cock rubbed against her hip. Heat flared through her, and her gaze flew to his. Arousal turned his honey-colored eyes dark. Gabby circled around behind her, and the heat from his body caused little shocks of awareness to ripple over her skin. Her heart pounded with excitement, butterflies danced through her belly, and her pussy clenched in anticipation. He settled his hands on her hips, and her nerve endings jumped to attention— waiting. Slowly, he gripped the bottom of her tank top and slid it up. She didn't stop him. Up her abdomen and torso, the material caught on her breasts for a moment before plunging over them. Her tits jiggled a little from the force. He pulled her shirt over her head and let it fall to the floor.

Boone watched them, his arms folded across his chest. Her nipples hardened under his scrutiny, pebbling into turgid little points. She really wished he would play with them. Tweak them. *Something.* But he just watched her, causing her breaths to come in little pants.

Gabby took hold of her hips with his big hands, and she jumped a fraction. This little striptease they were doing to her was torture—pleasant, arousing torture. He tugged on her sleeping pants and they slithered down her legs, leaving her only in her panties. Then he moved her hair aside and kissed her neck. A quiver of longing rushed through her. No matter how many times she fucked her men, she wanted more. Gabby swept her up in his arms and laid her on the bed. He moved away and Boone touched her leg, first on her knee then gently stroking upward. He crouched over her and settled his mouth on her mound, breathing against the thin cotton until the moisture from his breath dampened the material.

She squirmed, wanting him to do more. In response, he took her panties and shucked them off her quickly. She lay before them both like a sacrifice to the gods, with her legs spread wide and her body on display. Boone slid one finger between her slippery pussy lips and teased her clit in small circles. She gasped and arched her back. Gabby, who sat at her head, cupped her breasts. A jolt ran through her as his calloused hands caressed her softer flesh, the roughness sending bolts of electricity straight to her pussy. It was almost too much, the dual sensation of being stimulated by two sets of hands, two mouths, knowing that soon she would have two cocks pleasuring her as well.

Gabby kissed her, placing his firm lips over hers, teasing them apart until he waltzed his tongue inside to dance with hers. Kaiya inhaled his scent, an intoxicating blend of male and raw sexuality. Then he broke the kiss to nuzzle her neck and left little love bites everywhere. She didn't care that he marked her. Everything was intensified by the fact that Boone had lowered his face to her swollen folds then swiped his long tongue through her slit. He pushed one thick finger into her cunt as he gently sucked the sensitive little clit, finger-fucking steadily before adding a second finger to pump in and out. He slowly drove her out of her mind as a thunderous climax abruptly crashed through her, leaving her head to spin from the unexpected euphoria singing through her blood.

When Boone pulled his finger away, he held it up to her lips and she immediately sucked the digit into her mouth, swallowing the juices down. Boone's eyes glittered with approval and he stood up to take off his own clothing. The black T-shirt hid his muscles, which rippled as the shirt came over his head. She admired his tattoos for a moment before he pushed his jeans off his hips and stood before her. His long cock curled upward, with pre-cum leaking steadily. Kaiya licked her lips, but he denied her the tasty treat. Instead, he lined up his cock with her pussy, circled her waist with his hands, and thrust into her.

Even though she was soaked, his invasion took her breath away. Their gazes met, held, and he kept still until she adjusted to his girth. Then he leaned forward to cover her body with his and took one nipple gently between his teeth. Gabby did the same to her other nipple and Kaiya's senses blew apart as she threw back her head and groaned at the sensation of having both breasts sucked at the same time by two different mouths. She ran a hand through Boone's short hair and gripped the back of Gabby's longer locks, pressing them both closer to her breasts. Gabby was slightly more aggressive, giving small love bites on her aching nipple with his teeth then soothing it with his tongue.

Boone gyrated his hips, pulling out of her pussy only to ease back in slowly, almost as an afterthought as he lavished her nipple. Little by little, his speed increased until he pushed away and levered himself on his hands, which forced more of his cock deeper into her pussy. She gasped and could only hold on as he threw his head back, a magnificent beast ready to fuck her hard and deep. He bottomed out, his balls slapping against her as he hammered into her cunt. He pounded deep, causing the bed to bounce. Gabby had retreated from her breasts, but all she could focus on was Boone. Higher and higher, her body coiled until a finger pressed against her clit and she spiraled out of control, moaning, pushing, pulling, coming apart at the seams.

Boone's cock swelled, and he thrust one last time, burying all the way as his hot cum filled her. He rested his forehead on her shoulder, a slick coat of sweat covering him. Just as she was about to wrap her arms around him, he eased away. His cock slipped out of her, and a rush of juices poured out of her channel. Then she looked up as Gabby suddenly appeared. Kaiya didn't know if she had it in her for a second, but when he pushed his big cock into her, Kaiya's body lit up again. She hadn't quite come down from her previous orgasm, so the sensation kept her hovering on the brink as Gabby drove his dick deeper and deeper. He wasn't as finely finessed as Boone, but she adored his raw lovemaking. They rocked together, and she locked her legs tightly about his hips. Every thrust had him hitting her clit and it didn't take long for another climax to rip through every fiber of her sweaty body. She cried out in bliss just as Gabby shuddered in his own completion. He thrust into her one last time as his cum shot out to mingle with the combination of her and Boone's cream.

His heart thumped heavily against her chest and just as she reached out to cuddle with him, he abruptly left her to walk into the bathroom. Her arms were cold and empty and all she could do was stare in confusion as he shut the door without once looking at her. Then Boone was there, lifting her up and striding through the connecting door. He laid her down on her own bed and smoothed a lock of hair off her cheek.

"Why don't you go shower?" he suggested.

"What was that about?" she signed.

Boone compressed lips into a straight line. "I need to take care of Gabby and then I'll come back and spend the night with you."

"Why can't both of you sleep with me?"

Hesitation crossed his face. A secret, she thought. These two men didn't trust her with their secrets. With a non-committal shake of his head, Boone left her and closed the door behind him. On autopilot, she rose and headed for her bathroom. Showering, as he'd suggested. After she'd dried and donned a sleeping shirt and panties, Kaiya climbed between the cool sheets of the bed, but couldn't fall asleep. It was some time later that the door opened again and Boone came into the room. He stood for a moment over the bed, staring at her, so she didn't pretend to be asleep. She turned over to look at him, holding out a hand to invite him next to her. Without a word, he disrobed and slid in next to her. He pulled her into his arms and she rested her head upon his muscled chest.

Although she loved the intimacy, she couldn't help but think there was something missing. Her gaze strayed to the closed, locked door that led to the other room.

Gabby.

Chapter Ten

Kaiya drifted out of sleep and slowly opened her eyes as she stretched her dormant muscles. She reached for Boone, but found herself alone in the bed and sat up quickly. The muted light filtering around the edge of the curtains suggested it wasn't quite dawn. The connecting door stood open, so she rose and dressed in her sleep clothes before heading into the other room.

Boone and Gabby sat at the table, tall cups of store-bought coffee rested in their hands. Since Boone had his back to her, she couldn't read his lips, so she followed along the conversation with Gabby.

"Not sure if she'll go for it." Gabby shook his head. "Hell, no. It's your idea, so you have to execute it." Gabby shrugged. "What I want is irrelevant. But I do want her safe, so if you want to send her back to Bair, I'll stand by you."

She slapped the door, hard enough to make her palm throb. Both men turned, startled. Fiercely, she shook her head no.

"You don't understand, Kaiya," Boone said. Shame blazed in his eyes. "We were ambushed, and when the shooting died down, Cipher ran from it. He's still out there."

"And he's not working alone," Gabby added.

She frowned and signed, "Who is he working with?"

"We don't know," Boone said. "That's why we want you to go home to Bair. We want you to be safe."

Kaiya rubbed her eyes. Yes, the smart thing would be to leave, let Boone and Gabby handle this task. But that would also mean giving up this road trip before it had even begun, and the need to *live* far outweighed the threat of danger. All she kept imagining was the smirk on her grandfather's face that he was proven right, that she wasn't ready to be in the real world. That she should be back behind the high walls of her family's ancestral home. Looking at Gabby and Boone, they expected her to make the right choice. To agree. To *leave*. After all, she was always the sensible one. The demure one. The one who never put up a fight, or disagreed.

God, she sounded pathetic, even to herself.

Slowly, she shook her head. She couldn't be that girl anymore, even if the decisions she made were the wrong ones. The area between Gabby's eyes deepened as he frowned, but even under his obvious displeasure, she knew she couldn't tuck her tail and run back home.

"I understand the danger," she signed. "But I am *not* going back to Bair."

"Cipher is desperate," Gabby signed back. "And desperate men do unpredictable things."

She nodded, acknowledging that. "But I don't know how unpredictable *I* can be. Don't send me to hide, Gabby. You have no idea what it's like to be trapped. Caged without knowing if you are going to live or die behind walls."

He recoiled as if slapped, and she blinked at his response. The emotions on his face blazed from white-hot anger to hatred, only to burn to shameful embers. The life bleached out of his honey-colored orbs before he rose and left. He didn't look back as he opened the door and walked away. She didn't hear the door slam, but she saw Boone wince slightly and knew Gabby was beyond pissed.

Kaiya raised her hand, as if that would get him to stay, but Boone shook his head.

"No," he said as she read his lips. "Leave him be."

"What happened?" she signed.

"Nothing, except the fact that you know nothing about him." He ran a hand through his hair. "Get your things together. We'll head to Omaha and we'll decide there whether or not to send you home."

He turned to do his own packing, and she noticed he grabbed his and Gabby's saddlebags. She'd been dismissed—and it stung. In a span of a few minutes, she'd lost both of her men. Confused, she went back to her room and tried very hard not to hyperventilate with panic. She didn't want what they had to end. Not now.

Not ever.

* * * *

Gabby wished he'd grabbed the pack of cigarettes from the table because he really needed a nicotine fix. Smoking wasn't something he normally indulged in since he'd quit a few years back, but every once in a while he needed the hard bite of nicotine flooding his system. Even the action of lighting one up was calming. There was something about drawing the smoke deep into his lungs that soothed him.

Kaiya had no idea just how wrong she was. He knew very well the madness of being trapped in a cage. The fear. The stench. How hope felt when it died. The memories haunted him. Drove him to the point of insanity. During the day he could keep himself occupied, distracted, so he wouldn't remember what he'd done to survive. Boone understood. His club Brother knew firsthand what ghosts lingered in his subconscious. There wasn't another soul on Earth he trusted, although something inside told him that he could trust Kaiya. What was more, he *wanted* to include her in his life. Simple fucking wasn't the same thing as sharing everything, and he'd reached that point where he wanted an old lady.

But would she still want him once she learned what he'd done? Gabby looked at his hands. He'd stained with blood, and not the blood from those who actually deserved to die. No, his shame came from the death of innocent men.

The door to the room opened, and he glanced over to see Boone carrying both saddlebags. He reached for his and nodded his thanks.

"We'll be heading out in a few minutes," Boone murmured.

"Yeah," he said.

"It's only going to take us about an hour to get to Omaha. Figured we'll eat when we hit the city limits."

"Fine."

"Going to be monosyllabic now?"

"Maybe."

Boone snorted. "She didn't know what she was saying."

"Yeah." He sighed. "I want to tell her."

Boone frowned. "Everything?"

Gabby nodded. "I think we could build a life with her."

"Me too," Boone said softly. "She's a good woman. Smart. Sexy. Compassionate. She'd understand, Gordon."

"I hate it when you use my real name."

"I use your real name when you need reminding that what happened then doesn't define who you are now."

Gabby rubbed the back of his neck and gave a one-shoulder shrug. He may pretend like he didn't care, but Boone saw through his tough-guy act. The care and acceptance pouring from him was almost enough to bring tears in his eyes. Luckily, he was saved from showing too much emotion when the second door opened, and Kaiya emerged, wearing her brand new leather jacket. He smelled the leather aroma all the way to his bike.

She smiled tentatively at them, and Gabby's heart thumped excitedly in his chest. She may have stated some things without thought, but he'd never hold that against her. Kaiya had no clue to his military history and he needed to tell her about it if they were to have a future together. He'd never had such a lingering reaction to a woman, and it was more than just the fantastic sex. There was something about her that called to him on a primitive level. He wanted to protect her. Love her. Give her everything she wanted.

"Come on," Boone said, though he faced her so she could read his lips. "We'll have breakfast in Omaha."

Chapter Eleven

It only took an hour to reach Omaha, and by the time they stopped at a diner for breakfast, the sun had defeated the lingering chill of the night air. Boone took hold of Kaiya's hand as they made their way into the cozy warmth of the small restaurant, where the smell of eggs, bacon and coffee had her belly rumbling. She kept looking toward Gabby, but either he couldn't hear the mental S.O.S. she threw his way, or he was avoiding her.

They sat in a booth with Boone sliding in next to her while Gabby sat across. The waitress smiled in greeting, but the tired lines around her eyes hinted she'd been working too many long hours.

"Howdy, folks," she said, setting down three small glasses of water. "My name is Wanda. What's your poison?"

"Definitely coffee," Boone replied. "For all three of us."

She winked at him. "Coming right up. Menus are behind the napkin holder."

Kaiya grabbed one and grimaced as her fingers encountered a sticky mess on one side. She wiped her fingers, using the water from the glass to help clean them. By the time Wanda came back with three coffees and a bowl of creamers, Kaiya decided against the pancakes. One sticky go-round a day was enough.

They ordered their meals, and Wanda hurried away, sticking the ticket on the rotating cylinder in the kitchen window before moving onto the next table. Gabby and Boone both took their coffee black, but she added creamer after creamer, until the liquid was flush against the rim of her mug. Then she bent over to sip it without moving, because one jolt would have the sloshed brew all over the counter top.

Kaiya placed all the empty creamer containers back into the little dish, and when she looked at them, pleased with how diluted her coffee was, it was to encounter their shocked gazes. She pursed her lips and reached into her backpack for a pen and notebook.

"I don't like the bitter aftertaste of coffee, so I put a little cream in it."

"A little?" Gabby asked once he read her note. A smirk lingered at the corners of his mouth. "I think you just drained a whole cow dry."

The waitress returned with her arms loaded with plates and delivered the food with a flourish only years of experience could produce. They ate without fanfare, not looking at one another as they shoveled food into their mouths. Kaiya personally thought the food had tasted better at the diner where they'd had their first date, but it was hard to screw up bacon and eggs so she simply added more salt. When they were done, Boone waved to get her attention.

"I think we should go to the bus depot now and grab the contents of the locker."

"Why?" she wrote.

"Throw Cipher and his partner off guard." Boone finished his coffee.

Kaiya wrote quickly and held up her note. "Then I should get it. They'll be expecting two bikers, but not a woman."

"Cipher knows what you look like," Gabby replied.

She shrugged. "I can put on sunglasses to hide that I'm Japanese."

Boone shook his head. "It's too dangerous."

Anger threatened to flare again, but she took a deep, calming breath. Boone was the V.P. of a motorcycle club. He was used to giving orders, not taking them. It was time she learned how to maneuver around his decisions.

"It's easy to be in and out in five minutes," she wrote. "If Cipher is watching, I can quickly slip by, grab the contents in the locker and be gone before he or they realize what has happened."

"Kaiya, we wouldn't be inside the station to protect you."

"I can protect myself." When she saw that fact hadn't sold him, she pressed on. "Please don't think I'm incapable just because I'm deaf."

He ran a hand through his hair. "I've never once thought you incapable, Kaiya."

"Ever since my abduction, I've only made myself stronger," she wrote. "I know how to shoot, how to fight. I can be an asset to you."

He covered her pen, halting her words. She thought he was going to dismiss her like everyone else, but instead, he nodded. A huge smile graced her face, but he held up a finger.

"You will have ten minutes and you go in armed. All right?"

She nodded, acquiescing. Every piece of freedom or adventure she could grasp only made her wings spread a little wider. Luckily, Boone and Gabby finally seemed to understand that she didn't need coddling. They stood, and Boone went to pay for their meal before they headed out.

As Kaiya slipped on her helmet, she saw two bikers across the street watching them. One held a cigarette, and a plume of smoke curled upward only to disappear into the cool breeze. She tapped Boone's shoulder and nonchalantly nodded toward them. Boone tensed, letting her know he'd spotted them. The two bikers didn't move, only sat there observing as they mounted and rode off. Omaha was a beautiful city, thriving with new construction and the hustle and bustle of a metropolis. They headed out of the downtown area into the less developed neighborhood until they came to the busy bus station.

The depot was a lot larger than Lincoln's, taking up the whole block. People rushed in and out of the doors, activity swimming all around the place. Boone and Gabby parked and Kaiya got off the back, her heart pumping with adrenaline.

"Who were those bikers?" she signed.

"Don't know," Boone said as he took her helmet from her. "They wore patches on their cuts, but I couldn't tell which club. The local MC in Omaha is the Whiskey Knights. Could've been them just making sure we don't trip over any toes."

Boone pulled her in close and took out one of his guns from his shoulder holsters to slip into her jacket pocket. The thing barely fit, so she had to wrap her hand around the handle.

"Are you okay with the gun?" he asked.

She read his lips and nodded.

"You know how to use it?" he asked again.

"Yes," she mouthed.

He nodded and eased back. Gabby stepped forward and handed her the locker key. She wished they no longer had the awkward tension between them and she vowed to fix it when this was over.

"Number twenty-six," Gabby said.

She nodded. She remembered each locker number, totally random without any logic to them at all. Her mind spun over to Cipher's code, and she frowned. Maybe the locker numbers were just coincidence, but so far, nothing about Cipher was turning out to be cut and dried. From taking apart his office and going through his books, he may look a mess, but she'd learned he was a methodical plotter.

The bus station had people moving to and fro, hurrying in all directions, which made her a feel a bit better. There were so many people and she blended in as one more person milling about, especially with her backpack on. The sunglasses had belonged to Gabby, and she'd bent them so they'd stay firmly planted on her face. She looked around, heart pounding with fear, expecting to see Cipher jumping out at her like he'd done in the hardware store, but no one paid her any attention. She was just another nobody in the crowd.

The key burned in her pocket, so she hurried to the section that housed the lockers. The smaller numbers were in back, leaving the higher numbers as the first ones she approached. Wouldn't a man wanting to stuff a random duffel bag just go to the first locker? Why seek out a specific locker? As Kaiya went past the numbers—sixteen, fifteen, fourteen—her mind replaced the numbers with letters of the English alphabet. P was the sixteenth letter, O was the fifteenth… The twenty-sixth letter was Z. Locker number ten had been in

Lincoln. Number twenty-six in Omaha. Number six in Sioux City. Which would be JZF. Had Cipher picked these lockers based on something specific? Maybe his own initials? That sounded farfetched, but damned if the thought didn't persist. She'd have to ask Boone and Gabby when she returned.

Locker twenty-six looked untouched. Glancing to make sure no one was around, she pulled the key out of her pocket and hurried forward. The key slid into the lock with ease. Kaiya released a pent-up breath she hadn't realized she'd been holding. She turned the key and the door opened effortlessly. Inside lay another duffel bag. Without looking inside, she slung it over her shoulder, turned, and hurried back the way she had come.

She almost ran the entire way back, weaving in and out of the crowd, moving as quickly as possible. She was almost to the door when she saw a biker out of the corner of her eye. Kaiya halted and gasped as her gaze met the stare of the man from the diner. He watched her, without even bothering to try to hide himself, studying her as if she were some sort of curious specimen. Even behind the tinted shade of her glasses, their eyes locked, and terror flooded through her. Was this man helping Cipher? Was she being tracked even now? The questions had her snapping out of her shocked trance. She ran through the door, all the way to where Boone and Gabby stood by their bikes waiting on her. Her breath came in shocked little pants as Boone flung his arms around her.

"What happened?" Gabby signed. Even in sign language she could tell he was tense and on edge.

"One of the men from the diner was inside, watching me," she signed back.

Gabby turned around and stepped toward the entrance, but Boone's big chest rumbled so she assumed he'd told Gabby no. The two men shared a grim look, then Boone tugged on her arm, hurrying her to mount up. She had barely put on her helmet before they roared away from the bus station, riding hard and fast.

They maneuvered through the city, all of it a blur, until Boone signaled toward a gas station and they pulled both bikes up toward a pump. Kaiya hopped off, waiting as the men filled their gas tanks.

"You think we're being followed?" Gabby asked Boone.

Before Boone could answer, both men tensed and looked behind them. It took a moment for Kaiya to feel the vibration of motorcycles on the ground, and by then, it was too late for them to do anything. Four bikes rumbled into the gas station, surrounding them, and Boone grabbed her arm to yank her behind him. Her stomach rolled, and she had a sinking feeling they weren't here for just a friendly little chat.

* * * *

Boone watched each rider, instantly recognizing Stone Cold, the president of the Whiskey Knights. The gray that threaded his hair and mustache gave him an almost dopy look, which belied the man's cunning. He was probably in his late fifties, but the years as a hardened biker and ex-con hadn't done the man any favors. Deep lines marred his face, crisscrossing like a road map. Nicotine stains bled from his teeth onto the corner of his lip. A tall, thin man, his cold black eyes could freeze a man to death.

Next to him sat the man from the diner, the one who had been watching Kaiya in the depot. Boone didn't know the younger man, but he still recognized a dangerous person when he saw one. This had the potential of turning ugly, so instead of reaching for his gun, he raised his hands slightly to show he wasn't about to make a bad mistake.

"Boone," Stone Cold greeted him.

"Stone Cold. We don't want any trouble," Boone said.

"You come into my territory without permission, wearing your colors," Stone Cold said, shrugging. "That's not very friendly."

"We're just passing through. We meant the Whiskey Knights no disrespect."

Stone Cold kicked out his bike stand and propped his machine before dismounting. He walked around them, studying each in a slow, measured dose. Boone stayed still, although he wondered if he was making a colossal mistake not arming himself. If it wasn't for the fact that he was Kaiya's only shield and that they stood next to a fucking gas pump, he would've reached for his gun already. As it was, all he could do was wait.

"The Men of Hell, eh?" Stone Cold snorted. "Then you must know Bizerk and Vicious."

Boone jerked. "What the hell did you just say?"

"You heard me." Stone Cold stopped in front of him.

Boone glanced at the men boxing them in. They hadn't drawn their guns, but he doubted a little thing like shooting next to a gas line would stop them if he made a move on their president.

"Vicious and Bizerk are fucking psychos," he said.

"I won't argue that. They didn't like being stuck in the lower ranks of this club. Said they were going to form their own."

"The motherfuckers *didn't* form their own," Boone growled. "They tried stealing mine. They killed two of my Brothers. Almost killed my president's old lady."

"I heard about your club being targeted."

"Well, if you heard that and, if you know where Vicious is, then I demand you tell me!"

Stone Cold got right in his face, toe to toe, until all Boone saw was cold fury in his dark eyes. "First of all, I don't take orders from no one, least of all the V.P. of an inferior club. Second, I know what those two asses did to your club, which is the only reason I haven't put bullets in your head for trespassing. I knew the Men of Hell would come one day, which is why I had Eagle looking out for you. Seems like I have some restitution to pay out since they were *my* men."

He motioned with his hand, and the biker who'd been watching them stepped forward.

"This is Eagle," Stone Cold said. "He's the scout for the Knights. Tell them what you saw the other night."

"Happen to spot Vicious at the bus depot," Eagle replied. "Don't know what he was doing, but he was riding with a bald-headed man. Glasses. Skinny as fuck."

Boone shared a grim look with Gabby. "Yeah," he said, turning back. "We know him. Our old accountant."

Stone Cold folded his arms across his chest. "Why would your old accountant be riding with Vicious?"

Boone stared at the gathered Whiskey Knights. They seemed to have no compunction of starting a gunfight next to a highly explosive substance. *Shit.* He turned to Kaiya and gestured for the duffel bag. She took it off and he tossed it over. It landed with a thunk at Stone Cold's feet.

The man looked at him suspiciously before bending to open it. He looked surprised as he held up one of the stacks of cash.

"This is a lot of fucking money," he said.

"He stole it from our club," Boone replied.

Stone Cold tossed the stack back into the duffel and zipped it shut. When he stood, he had a firm hold on the bag. "We could consider this to be a good will gesture on your part."

Of course. "As I see it, you lost control of your men, who came and killed two Men of Hell members. I fail to see what goodwill gesture I'm responsible for."

Stone Cold glared at him for a long, tense moment. Then he grinned and tossed the duffel bag to Eagle. "You'll come to the clubhouse, stay with us while we show you our apology. Then we'll talk about your toll for entering my territory."

Boone sighed. *Fuck.*

Chapter Twelve

Gabby didn't like this, not one bit.

He followed Stone Cold and Eagle, with two other Whiskey Knights riding behind them forming a stifling cage around them. He kept glancing at Boone, wanting the man to veer off suddenly so they could get the hell away from this MC. Deep down, he knew that wasn't an option, but that was why Boone was V.P. and he was just fucking muscle. It wasn't that he was dumb, but he simply didn't have the temperament to go down the politics path, and sitting at the head of the table was nothing but weighing the pros and cons of action. Office material he was not.

The Whiskey Knights compound was located out of the city, on a ranch for crying out loud—green rolling hills, white picket fences and horses that dotted the horizon. Not to mention the fact that there was no one to hear any gunshots, as well as having lots of places to hide a body. It was enough to mess with Gabby's carefully controlled emotions as the main gate closed behind them with a loud clang.

Stone Cold led them down a paved, winding driveway past the picturesque three-story house to the outlaying barns, where about fifty Harley's all stood in neat little rows. Two additional barns in the distance had armed guards at the door, holding nice little AR-15s that would fuck someone up real good. It didn't take a genius to figure out that was where the real money for the Whiskey Knights was cooking—literally.

Men mingled around a bonfire, drinking, even though it was before noon. Women, some old ladies and some sweet butts, dressed in all forms of provocative outfits hung around the fringe. The sweet smell of marijuana wafted on the soft breeze. They had more than one pair of eyes trained on them and it made Gabby's skin itch.

Stone Cold parked his bike and kicked out the stand. Gabby and Boone followed his example as the rest of the Whiskey Knights pulled around them, blocking them. He saw Eagle staring at Kaiya once again as she dismounted from behind Boone and took off her helmet, shaking her black hair free. He had the urge to go over and pound the shit out of the fucking scout, which would probably be detrimental to staying alive, seeing he was vastly outnumbered. No doubt the other members would take exception to him killing one of their own.

Above all, he had to watch out for Kaiya. He didn't trust any of the Knights.

"Come," Stone Cold said, waving at them. "Let's talk."

Boone closed his hand around Kaiya's as they followed the president. He was a tall man, walking with a noticeable limp to his left leg. All the members greeted him as he parted the tribe, much like Moses had done with the Red Sea.

"Starting the celebration a little early, eh?" Boone asked.

"Most of the men just came back from a successful run." Stone Cold winked. "Very prosperous."

They made their way up a dirt path that led to the house. Stone Cold opened the back door and entered, gesturing for them to follow. Eagle snapped the screen door shut behind them. Gabby glared at him and maneuvered so the other man wasn't at his back. He didn't like being so vulnerable.

The kitchen was big and bright, with the rich smell of lemon disinfectant lingering in the air. A young blonde woman stood at the sink, washing dishes and, when she glanced up, a shriek of happiness erupted from her. She threw down the sponge to bolt over to Stone Cold. He braced himself as the petite woman threw herself in his arms and slapped her mouth against his for a deep kiss. As they came up for air, the age difference was glaringly obvious. If the woman was legal, Gabby knew it was probably by the skin of her teeth.

Stone Cold disentangled himself from the blonde and turned toward them with a shit-eating grin on his face. "This is Lisa," he said. "My soon to be old lady. Lisa, make sure you treat these men real nice. They're special guests of the Whiskey Knights."

"Men of Hell, eh?" she said, giving him and Boone a onceover before her gaze rested on Kaiya. "Are you an old lady?"

Kaiya shrugged in a generic sort of way. She didn't want to be rude, but she also didn't want to play up she could read lips or communicate.

Boone took up the introductions. "I'm Boone. This is Gabby. And this is Kaiya."

Stone Cold nodded down a hallway and led down them toward the front of the house. Wooden planks creaked under foot, reverberating loudly. Boone held onto Kaiya's hand just as Stone Cold held Lisa's. The large farmhouse had been modified for the club's need, and Stone Cold opened a door to a sealed off room to reveal their chapel. Several club Brothers stood watch just outside the screen door and they greeted Stone Cold with a nod of respect.

Stone Cold pointed at Kaiya. "This is an official meeting. She can go with Lisa."

"Kaiya stays by my side," Boone said in a tone that booked no argument. He was taller than Stone Cold by a few inches and greatly out muscled him. "She's deaf and won't hear a word of what happens inside Church. But she doesn't leave my side."

Stone Cold looked from him to Gabby and back. He wasn't happy with Boone's declaration. "Deaf, eh?"

Boone simply turned to Kaiya and signed. "Nonmembers don't sit in Church, especially women. But I don't trust them and I don't want you being alone here."

"Aren't they your allies?" she asked with her hands.

"Not really," he replied.

"All right," Stone Cold said. "I get it. She can't fucking hear." He looked at Eagle. "You have a problem with her inside?"

Eagle shook his head.

Stone Cold kissed Lisa on the lips and patted her ass back toward the kitchen before opening the chapel doors. Lisa lingered for a moment, staring at Kaiya, before turning and walking away. Church was the formal dining room, or at least it had been once upon a time. A china hutch still resided against one wall, but instead of dishes, ammunition filled it. Next to it was a safe and a wall of weapons. Gabby had to admit, the guns were beautiful, everything from nine millimeters to Ak-47s. There was even a grenade launcher. The ATF would have a field day with the collection.

"Sit," Stone Cold ordered. He stood behind the head chair and stared at them. Eagle and another man pulled out chairs on either side of him. Gabby waited until his V.P. and Kaiya sat before taking his own seat at the opposite end of the Whiskey Knights' table.

"Warm fuzzies aside, why exactly have you brought us to your compound?" Boone asked, getting the ball rolling immediately.

Stone Cold nodded to the duffel bag that Eagle laid upon the table. "I'll give you about a hundred thousand reasons."

"The money belongs to the Men of Hell."

Stone Cold spread his arms. "And yet you're at the hospitality of the Whiskey Knights."

Gabby snorted. Eagle shot him a dark look before glancing back over to Kaiya, which didn't help Gabby's mood at all.

"You have a beautiful compound," Boone said diplomatically. "But we're on a run ourselves and really need to move on."

"And I wish to talk potential business," Stone Cold said.

"Business?" Boone asked.

Stone Cold threaded his fingers and cracked them before settling his hands on his belly. "I propose a working relationship with the Men of Hell."

"What could we possibly have that the Knights would want?" Boone asked. "Besides the hundred grand, of course."

"The Men of Hell have a lucrative spot along Interstate 80. Now, I know your cashbox is hurting, so I'm very interested in making a deal to pass through your territory."

"You interested in Colorado or Wyoming?"

"Colorado."

"Good," Boone said. "Keeps you out of our territory. The Men of Hell have trade in Wyoming."

Stone Cold nodded. "I'm well aware of your relationship with the Red Wolves."

"The Red Wolves are out of the drug-running business."

"So I've heard," Stone Cold replied. "Human trafficking. Nasty business all around. Not that I'm feeling the loss of the Demon Devils."

Boone snorted. "Yeah, neither are we. So this trade route you're looking for, you could easily pass right by Bair via the interstate. Free range. No need to involve us."

"I was hoping we could become business associates," Stone cold said. "Since you have Wyoming you can easily take our product into that market."

"What's your product?"

"Meth. Figured since you're now in business with Red Eye we could be copacetic. We mule for you and you can mule for us. We'll both increase our revenue and product services."

Boone crinkled his brow. Gabby remembered two barns guarded far away from anything else. Pretty smart, being on private property as well as putting the dangerous kitchen away from any other building. If there were an accident, the only people who would die would be the chef, his minions, and maybe a prospect or two. Gabby wasn't sure if getting involved with another club would be beneficial, but that's why he wasn't the one making the decisions.

"Romeo will want to talk with you," Boone said. "It's subject to a club vote, and that I can't guarantee would be yes."

"You can back it," Stone Cold said. "And to show my gratitude, as well as my apologies for Vicious and Bizerk, please stay with us while we celebrate our Brother's return."

"You know Bizerk is dead, right?" Boone said.

The Knights stared at them in shock.

"No," Stone Cold said slowly. "I hadn't heard. Who did it?"

Gabby tensed. "Does it matter?"

Slowly, the Whiskey Knights' president shook his head. "No. Vicious and Bizerk left their cuts behind when they hightailed it out of here, traitors to their colors. I would've shot them on sight."

"You killed him, didn't you?" Eagle asked, looking straight at Boone.

"I didn't have a choice," Boone replied coldly. "He was going to kill me."

"Not to mention the fact that he and your other fucking reject chopped up one of our prospects and blew up our fucking bar," Gabby snapped. He rarely said anything in meetings, but the whole situation rubbed him the wrong fucking way.

"Well, you killing Bizerk might account for why Vicious is suddenly back," Eagle said blandly. "Following you."

"You mean revenge."

"Yeah, 'cause you killed the love of his life."

Now it was their turn to stare in shock.

"Come again?" Gabby asked. "They were gay?"

"Nah," Eagle said. He reached in his pocket and brought out a pack of cigarettes. He pulled one out, stuck it in his mouth and lit it with a lighter. "At least Bizerk wasn't. I'm not too sure of Vicious. The man fucked pussy, but I do know he had an unhealthy obsession with Bizerk."

"Shit," Boone muttered as he glanced quickly at Kaiya.

Gabby could read the worry on his V.P.'s face. If Vicious wanted revenge, there wasn't anything better than an eye for an eye.

"Enough talk about Vicious," Stone Cold said. He pushed the duffel bag toward Boone. "I'm not going to insist on a toll as a token of good faith. Stay the day and night. The last room on the third floor is yours. Eat, drink, and fuck any sweet butt you'd like. You can even sample our product if you wish, to make sure it's top quality shit."

The Whiskey Knights chuckled among themselves, and as the meeting broke up, everybody rose to resume the party outside. Gabby caught Eagle staring once more at Kaiya.

He cracked his knuckles.

Chapter Thirteen

Kaiya wasn't sure how to process the conversation that had happened in the meeting. She'd gotten most of it, missing only a few things when she couldn't see someone's lips. The Whiskey Knights were very different from the Men of Hell — darker, scarier. The compound seemed to have been a farm at one time. The untended fields lay fallow and overgrown. Now it was a fortified fortress that looked a lot like her grandfather's estate in Los Angeles — the men, the guns, the sense of danger lurking everywhere. The differences came in minute details, like the drugs on blatant display. The sickly sweet smell of weed lingered in the air. Even the more hardcore drugs like crack and heroin were being passed around in small circles. Many women were undressed, showing more tits and ass than she'd ever seen in her life. There were even couples fucking out in the open. Her grandfather would've never allowed such open sexual behavior.

Did the Men of Hell party like this? The few times she'd walked into that part of the clubhouse, she'd not seen this type of behavior. Had they and Chloe been sheltering her from this side of gang life? Or were the Men of Hell a different type of club altogether?

She didn't like the fact that once again someone seemed to be babying her, as if she were capable of breaking. What would it take to prove she was strong? Worthy of being trusted and part of club life? Hell, she didn't even *know* what it meant to be part of the club life. She tugged on Boone's hand. When he looked at her, she signed that she had to use the restroom. He glance over her head to Stone Cold and asked for her. Even though she read the answer on the other man's lips, she still waited for Boone to direct her. She had a feeling she shouldn't reveal too much to this man.

"Second floor, first door on the right."

"I'll wait for you," Gabby signed.

She shook her head and told him she'd be right back. He didn't like that, and she could tell by way he furrowed his brow, but she needed a moment. As she walked away, the stares of the men stayed on her back.

She lingered in the bathroom as she took care of business and washed up as best as possible — collecting herself. No use getting worked up over a possibility, especially since they were pilgrims in an unholy land. When she opened the door to exit, Eagle leaned against the opposite wall, arms folded over his chest as he waited. She blinked, suddenly unsure under his bold gaze.

"I know you can read my lips," he said, straightening. "I see things and I knew you understood everything that was said in that meeting."

She lifted her chin.

"I'm not here to twist your panties." He smiled, although it was more predatory than anything else. "You with Boone?"

She nodded.

"Any chance he'd share you?"

She shook her head no.

"Are you sure?"

She walked away without answering and or looking back. She didn't trust these Whiskey Knights at all, and now she trusted Eagle even less. She could feel his stare on her back and she withheld the shudder of nervousness that coursed through her. Why was he following them? Was it true what he'd said about Vicious? She didn't know the man, since she'd come after he had shot Chloe, but she knew the story.

At the bottom of the stairs, she glanced where the club's chapel was located and saw Stone Cold talking covertly to the men who had been sitting in front of the television. He suddenly looked up and their gazes met. The man scared her. He'd clearly gotten his nickname from how emotionless, how soulless his black eyes were. She turned away and headed toward the kitchen. Lisa was still there, chopping vegetables. She smiled at Kaiya and held up a finger, halting her retreat. Lisa wiped her hands and grabbed a pen and small notebook from a drawer. She wrote something and held it up.

"Would you like something to eat or drink?"

Kaiya's first instinct was to say no, but her belly rumbled. It'd been a few hours since breakfast. She held her hand for the paper and pen and Lisa handed them over. "Eat. Thank you."

Lisa smiled and nodded. She headed to the refrigerator where she took out deli meats and cheeses. She made a ham sandwich then handed it over. Kaiya nodded her thanks and began to eat.

Lisa wrote out another note.

"You don't have to stay with the men. You can hang out with me."

Kaiya smiled, not quite sure what to do. What was the procedure here? Was she supposed to hang out with Lisa? Was this a men's only club situation? She gave a generic half shrug, half nod answer. Lisa went back to writing.

"I've heard about the M.O.H. A friend of mine is from Bair. The MC world is quite small, especially out here in the sticks."

Kaiya nodded. What could she say to that? She was new to the motorcycle club slash gang world. Lisa was young, but the calculating gleam in her eyes told a deep, darker story. The blonde turned away to grab a beer from the refrigerator. She opened it and set it down in front of Kaiya. Kaiya reached for it and saluted Lisa as thanks.

"You're very pretty," she wrote.

Kaiya smiled her way of thanks and took a long drink.

"How long are you and your men staying?"

Kaiya held out her hand and Lisa placed the pen and notebook in her hand. "I think we're leaving tomorrow."

"Going where?"

Kaiya frowned. Was Lisa pumping her for information for Stone Cold? "Sioux City."

She put down the pen and finished the sandwich, which had turned into a big ball of lead in her stomach. She didn't like Lisa's direct questions and wanted to get back to Boone's and Gabby's side. Grabbing her beer, she mouthed thank you and rose. With one last strained smile at Lisa, she exited out the back door. Once outside, she breathed easier and decided not to leave Gabby or Boone's side again. The shark-infested waters were too thick to navigate.

It took her a few minutes to find them in the sea of bodies. There were too many people to wade through, who stared at her with a mixture of curiosity and distrust. When she finally spotted both men, she saw Eagle next to them. She hesitated because she didn't relish being under his slimy scrutiny once more. Then, in the next instant, Gabby hauled off and hit Eagle square in the jaw. The man fell back, but he just smiled through the powerful blow, pushed to his feet and returned the hit. Panic flooded through her and she hurried forward, intent on breaking up the brawl, but Boone grabbed her about the waist to hold her back. Soon, most of the Knights were watching the two big men fighting it out. Eagle had blood running from his mouth while Gabby's cheek had been split. She screamed, but the futile sound was drowned out amidst the cheers and encouragement of the watching spectators. All she could do was wait until it was over.

* * * *

"What do you think?" Boone muttered to Gabby as they settled into the background with beers in their hands.

Gabby enjoyed a party like any other man, but it was hard to relax when they were surrounded by men wearing different colors. If the Whiskey Knights had been friends of the Men of Hell, it would be a completely different ball game. As it was, all he could do was try to ignore the unease twisting through him.

"I think everything Stone Cold said was a crock of shit," Gabby replied.

Boone nodded and took a sip of beer. "Me too. How did he know who our new supplier was? Or that we were flat broke?"

"A spy?" Gabby asked.

"I don't know," Boone said. "I thought Romeo took care of the traitors in our midst. But what's Stone Cold's angle?"

"That I don't know."

Eagle sidled up to them with a knowing smirk deforming his lips. Gabby was sick and tired of seeing the smug look on the man's face, as if he knew a secret everyone else didn't.

"So what 'cha think of the meeting?" Eagle asked.

Boone shrugged. "Still processing."

"Yeah. I understand. By the way, sweet little piece you have."

Gabby tensed.

"I'm sure you're talking about my bike," Boone replied coldly.

"No," Eagle replied breezily, as if he didn't recognize the danger presented in both of them. "I was talking about your piece of ass. I was wondering if you'd be willing to share her."

Gabby's fist flew instantly, smashing into the Knight's lip and splitting it. Eagle fell back, but he didn't stay down long. He jumped up and charged, and the brawl only escalated. Fists and blood flew. Vaguely Gabby heard someone shouting at him to stop, but he'd be damned if he'd quit until the fucking asshole lay unmoving on the ground. Eagle might not have been as muscular, but he definitely held his own, giving as good as he was taking. Soon everyone was watching, urging them on. Their cries of encouragement rang in his ears, trigging the memory of another fight. Another time. When he'd been forced to fight his countrymen or risk them being killed. For a second, everything faded around him, and he was back on the sand. Back in that fucked-up hellhole. Sickness snaked inside him and he stumbled back, staring in horror at Eagle, struggling to breathe.

Instead of charging, Eagle stared at him in confusion. Then he backed down. Gabby looked around, saw Kaiya staring at him with wide, terrified eyes, and disgust sluiced through him. It had happened again. The madness had taken over for an instant. Horrified, Gabby turned and hurried away, pushing through the throng of people waiting for the fight to resume. He left the area, grabbing some booze to help him through the night. He left Kaiya in Boone's care because she was better off with him. Boone wasn't the monster. He wasn't the one going crazy.

Gabby knew it was a matter of time until he lost his sanity for good. The madness never truly went away. He just wished he had the strength to end it all before he hurt someone he loved.

Like Kaiya.

Chapter Fourteen

Kaiya took a step after him, but Boone grabbed her arm and halted her. She frowned at him.

"He needs to be alone."

She shook her head.

"Listen, Kaiya," he said, placing both hands on her shoulder. "Gabby has problems and sometimes his way of dealing is by being alone. He would not want you with him right now. He doesn't want anyone with him. Including me."

He linked their fingers together and tugged her away from the spot where Gabby had disappeared. She kept glancing back until the throng of people closed around them and he was lost within a sea of bodies. The loss was monumental somehow, and she had a niggling feeling that this moment would be significant at some point down the line. It gave her a moment of pause as she contemplated if she was strong enough to handle whatever dark burden Gabby carried. After all, Chloe had shielded her from much of the messed-up situation of their family, and Kaiya was rapidly discovering that breaking free from the restrictions placed upon her meant facing a barrage of unknown emotions.

Someone must have turned the bass on or turned it up because it vibrated through the ground and caused some of the more scantily clad women to shake their assets. As they made their way through the throng of gyrating bodies and clouds of pot smoke, she realized Boone was well known among this group. Maybe it was respect for the patch he wore, the words Vice President white and bold upon his cut, or maybe it was the fact that he was just a big motherfucker. Men greeted him, and Boone socialized, a mask slipping over his face to be friendly to the natives. However, Kaiya could only think about Gabby. The look of fear and devastation on his face would haunt her for some time. She'd seen the same look upon Chloe's face a time or two. Gabby must have gone through something very traumatic to put such bleak hopelessness in his eyes. She wished she could hold him and reassure him that things would be better, but she had no idea what that could be since she didn't know his past. Was he keeping her out deliberately? She looked at Boone. Were they both blocking her out on purpose?

As the hours slipped by, she nursed the one beer Boone had handed her. Partly because she wanted to keep her wits about her but also because she didn't want to chance running into Eagle again at the restroom. She occasionally saw him mingling through the throng of people. His laser gaze didn't seem to miss anything, and she never saw alcohol in his hands. Every once in a while their eyes would meet, and her insides froze until she would press against Boone for a semblance of safety, but the truth of the matter was that something didn't sit well with this club. Her stomach cramped, and she couldn't shake the fact that all wasn't what it seemed.

At some point, she and Boone had ended up near the outskirts of the party, closer to one of the barns. Boone touched her shoulder, and she looked up at him.

"You are thinking so loud I can feel it."

She gave a ghost of a smile at his phrasing and signed back. "I am worried about Gabby. And I don't like this club."

He nodded. "I don't either," he signed back.

"Will you recommend them to Romeo for the collaboration?"

"Hell, no."

Night had fallen and a cache of wood was added to the bonfire, causing the flames to rise high. Firelight twirled around the dancers nearby, adding an element of sensuality to their writing bodies. In the sunlight, they had seemed garish, but the shadows flickering around them turned them into works of erotic art. Maybe it was all the alcohol flowing but with the darkness came a sense of carnal permission—freedom. Men and women engaged with all sorts of sexual acts, from blow jobs to outright fucking. Kaiya had watched porn on the Internet, but she'd never seen it on such display, live and in her face. At first, the blatant promiscuity was startling, but when Boone settled his hand on the nape of her neck, a shiver of awareness ran down her body at the control he wielded in his hands. He could easily wrap his fingers around her neck and strangle the breath from her body. He kissed her shoulder as he explored her body, moving his hand from her neck to roam down her waist and span around her hips. He pulled her back against his body and ground his very hard denim-clad cock into her ass. Desire flared through her, heart hammering in excitement. With Boone behind her, Kaiya stared at the debased revelry happening around them. It gave her a thrill to realize she was part of it, joining the others in voyeuristic pleasure.

As Boone continued his tender assault on her body, her arousal grew until her pussy throbbed with desire, wet and sensitive against the crotch of her jeans. The lust in front of her became an aphrodisiac. She couldn't look away from it as it drew her in with gossamer strings, trapping her in a sensual web of passion. Boone slid his hand down her pelvis to the fastening of her pants and deftly undid them enough so he could slip his hand inside. Featherlike strokes touched her at first as he parted her moist folds to find her clit. The little bud practically went up in flames when he rubbed it. He pushed one long finger inside her pussy, and she instantly clamped down to suck it deeper into her channel. God, she really wanted his cock to fill her up. Kaiya squirmed as Boone continued finger-fucking her and she rotated her hips more into his groin, relishing the hardness contained behind the zipper. In response, he added another finger and she couldn't help but rock against his hand, seeking the climax she so desperately craved.

Her gaze met the amused stare of Lisa, who stood next to her old man. Stone Cold seemed oblivious to Boone and Kaiya as he talked to some men, but Lisa never took her gaze away, and desire slammed through Kaiya so quick and hot that it burned her up. Voyeurism was a new kink and knowing that someone saw her go up in flames was an experience too wild to tame. As Boone sucked on the side of her neck, she splintered apart. She hurtled off the precipice, and loved the rush toward ecstasy that gained by the second. It was beyond reason, beyond will, beyond anything but sensation, made more lascivious by having Lisa watch her fly apart.

When she rode the quivers of her orgasm, Boone pulled his fingers from her pussy and offered them to her, glistening with her own wet juices. Keeping her eyes fixated on Lisa, Kaiya sucked each finger into her mouth one by one. Then Boone took her hand to drag her away into the darkness, and the connection to Lisa was broken.

She had no time to process that, however, as Boone pushed her against the side of the barn and kissed her, hard. She encircled his neck as the tension built once more through her body.

"Get your jeans off."

She read his lips when he broke the kiss and could only imagine the husky growl accompanying the words. He was already unzipping his own jeans. Kaiya couldn't move fast enough, awkwardly toeing off her boots as she pulled down her pants. She'd only just gotten one leg free when Boone tore her panties off with a mighty tug. He swept her up and pressed her back against the aluminum siding of the barn, using it to help support her as he reached between them and lined his cock up with her wet, aching pussy. Once the tip was seated just inside her channel, he grabbed her ass, held tight and surged forward, filling her in one deep thrust.

Both moaned at the exquisite feeling.

At any second they could be caught. Someone could walk around the side of the barn and see them on display, and the knowledge that they were out in the open sent a salacious thrill through her. Boone pounded into her, driving her pleasure up, but also seeking his own. This was raw, unfiltered fucking, and she loved it. Loved how the moonlight shown down upon them and made it all the more graphic.

Foreplay wasn't needed, not when she'd just been consumed with fire a moment ago. Need slammed hot and heavy through her. Kaiya grunted as Boone buried his cock into her, again and again. He was so big and hard and all she could do was hang on and let her orgasm rise quickly through her body. He pumped her rhythmically at first as he gripped her ass cheeks tightly and moved her up and down on his dick. She couldn't hold back the moan as his cock penetrated deep into her pussy. She shuddered as an orgasm swept through her body, and he increased his pace. Now he plunged harder, out of control, and a second later he stiffened in her arms as his hot cum flooded her. He rested his forehead against hers as he shook in the aftermath of bliss. He kissed her softly on the forehead, then he pulled away and tucked his softening cock back inside his pants

Kaiya panted as he bent to put her leg back into her jeans, not caring in the least that their combined juices ran down her thighs and dirtied her pants. He swept her up in his arms and marched back toward the house. He didn't stop, didn't look at anyone, just passed through the crowd of people still parting. He made a beeline for the house, up the stairs to their bedroom where he kicked the door closed soundly behind them.

* * * *

Stone Cold reclined in his comfortable chair as Lisa gave him a nice, fucking blow job. As she hollowed out her cheeks, sucking him down, he had to admire her technique. The young girl was certainly talented, which was the main reason he even had the remote thought of making her his old lady. Lisa was high maintenance but when she wrapped those pretty lips around his cock, his higher brain functions ceased to work properly and he was ready to walk down the fucking aisle.

His phone vibrated, and he was half inclined to ignore it, but he was the president of the club and if shit was going down somewhere he had to know. With a disgruntled sigh, he opened the cheap flip phone.

"What?" he growled.

Lisa tried to lift her head to stop, but he buried his fingers in her hair and pushed her firmly back down. She got the hint and deep throated him again.

"You fucking told me to do it," came a slurring voice.

Stone Cold pulled the phone away from his ear quickly to check the number — unlisted. "Vicious?"

There was a scuffle of noise, then Vicious mumbled, "You told me to leave."

"Jesus, are you drunk?"

Vicious snorted. "Fuck you. You're equally as guilty of Bizerk being dead."

"I never told you to attack another fucking club!"

"You told me I would never rise in the Knights."

"Because you don't have the temperament. Vicious... Fuck. Come home."

"Read my lips, you asshole. Fffffuck off." He laughed a little hysterically. "I've found the mother lode, you know. I've got me my own Man of Hell, and he's got a lot of fucking money."

Stone Cold remained silent, letting him ramble.

"And I'm going to destroy them, Stone Cold," Vicious said, hiccupping. "Boone is going to burn."

And with a maniacal laugh echoing through the connection, he abruptly ended the call. Stone Cold slowly sat the phone back on the table. He released

Lisa's head when he realized his dick had gone limp. She sat up and glared at him.

"You ass," she snapped. She pointed to his crotch. "Now we're both not going to get lucky tonight. Perhaps one of the drugs you should be peddling is Viagra—"

He gripped her around the throat. "Don't sass me, girl. You might be talented in many ways, but I won't hesitate to fuck you up if you disrespect me."

He tossed her away, and she quickly rose and stormed into the bathroom, slamming the door closed. Stone Cold winced. Great. No blow job now and a pissy woman to deal with.

Fucking Vicious.

* * * *

Boone cursed under his breath as he shoved his chilled hands in his jean pockets. He should be sleeping next to his woman, warm and toasty, instead of searching in the dark for Gabby. It was pitch black and the woods surrounding the far were massive, making the task hard as fuck. Gabby knew how to hide so he wouldn't be found if he didn't want to be. But Boone hoped the alcohol would dull those abilities so he could find his brother. The party had mostly died down, although there were a few men still tending the bonfire and a few others drinking.

When Gabby had grabbed the bottle of whiskey, Boone knew exactly what he was going to find. What he was going to have to deal with. It wasn't the first bender Gordon Dixon had gone on and it certainly wouldn't be the last, not unless the man decided to get help from the demons that plagued him.

Boone's foot connected with something heavy, and he stumbled. When he looked closer at what had snagged his balance, he saw a body in the dense dark underbrush of the surrounding forest. He sighed, grabbed hold of Gabby's leg and pulled, grunting because his friend was one big motherfucker. An empty whiskey bottle rolled away as fumes wafted up from the dead-drunk man. Boone sighed as he bent to try to rouse him. No way could he carry Gabby fireman style unless he had some help, so he slapped Gabby's face until the man moaned.

"Come on," he muttered. "Help me get you up."

Gabby tried to roll onto his side.

"On your feet, soldier!"

Gabby's eyes opened a fraction. "Yessss, sirrrr," he slurred.

Between the two of them, although Boone was doing a little more of the work, they got Gabby to his feet. He flung Gabby's arm across his shoulder and Boone hooked his own around his friend's waist. It was sheer dumb luck that he'd stumbled across the unconscious man, following the direction he'd last seen him go only a couple of hours before. He'd seen Gabby sneak back to get more alcohol and knew he needed space, that the fight had triggered memories that weren't as deeply buried as Gabby thought. Gabby pretended that they were, that he could handle them by locking himself away, but Boone knew better. The man was a wreck. Had been for years. Life in the MC had helped him suppress that part of himself, but every once in a while something triggered the self-destruction that had him locking Gabby up for his own protection. Tonight would be one of those nights.

The farm was large and it took them a while, stumbling along in the dark, to make their way back to the house. Several Whiskey Knights looked at them, but they probably figured Gabby was just another drunk. Boone knew better. He was one more soldier who would've succumbed to suicide had Boone not made it his mission to nurse Gabby through the nightmares.

He stumbled into the house and slowly up the stairs, silently cursing the fact that Stone Cold had given them a place on the third goddamn floor. He burst into the room and Kaiya gasped, bounding to her feet. She'd been reclining on the bed, reading from her tablet, but laid the device aside to help him. Together they got Gabby on the bed and removed his boots and jeans, trying to make him as comfortable as possible.

"I've never seen him like this before," she signed, looking down at Gabby.

"He was hoping you'd never see him this bad."

"Does he drink like this often?"

Boone shook his head. "Only when the ghosts walk through his memory."

"Ghosts?" she signed.

"There are many things you don't know about him."

He could tell she was curious and Boone knew it was a matter of time before they would have to tell her everything. Even though Kaiya had started this affair just wanting a good time, he had known she was something special. He wanted her in his life and he knew Gabby wanted her too. He sighed and ran a hand through his hair. Yes, that was one issue they were going to have to address soon because no way was he letting her go.

Gabby lay thrashing against the bed, sweating from the nightmare that gripped him in its greedy talons. She watched, confused at first, as Boone extracted something from his saddlebag and approached the bed. He brought Gabby's hands over his head and snapped some type of fleece-lined cuff around one wrist before winding it through the wrought-iron headboard. Then he secured the other wrist and yanked on the metal binds to make sure they were tight.

"What are you doing?" she signed.

Boone ignored her and grabbed something else from the saddlebag. In shock, she watched as he brought out a leather cord and bound Gabby's ankles. When he was done, Gabby looked like some trumped up Thanksgiving turkey, ready for carving.

Kaiya took a step toward him, but Boone prevented her from going closer. She shrugged off his hand and faced him.

"Take those cuffs off!" she signed angrily.

He shook his head. "No," he signed back. "I can't."

"Can't or won't?"

"Can't, Kaiya. He's been drinking, and combined with the fight with Eagle, he wouldn't want to hurt you."

"Hurt me?" She shook her head. "He'd never do that."

"Of course not," he said.

She could read the frustration etched in every line on his face.

"He never meant to hurt anyone. And he won't as long as he's tied up."

That brought her up short. She blinked at him. "He's hurt someone?"

Boone nodded. "Right after he became a prospect. I'd already been patched into the club. He… He had a flashback nightmare. Another prospect tried to help him, but Gabby beat him so badly he ended up in traction for months. Ever since that night, he's had me handcuff him to the bed."

Horrified, Kaiya stared at Gabby still tossing and turning on the bed, just now understanding the depth of how much this man had suffered. "He has PTSD," she signed. "He needs help. Therapy."

Boone touched her shoulder and when she looked at him, he nodded sadly. "He refuses."

"That's stupid," she signed back, frowning. "A man can't live his life chained up like an animal."

"This is what he chose to do."

"You say you're his friend, but a friend would get him help."

He frowned. "You are signing too fast."

She took a deep breath. "I'm going to sit next to him tonight."

"That's not a good idea."

"I do not care about what you think is a good idea." Kaiya signed slow enough to make sure he understood every word. "Is this why he won't spend the night with me?"

Boone nodded.

She couldn't believe this was the reason why Gabby refused to sleep next to her. "I am going to take care of him tonight."

She marched past him and sat on the edge of the bed. If he wouldn't remove Gabby's handcuffs, at least she could be with him to make sure he didn't hurt himself. Boone touched her shoulder and she frowned at him, feeling more than a little perturbed at him.

"He's my Brother, in more ways than one," Boone said. "I'd do anything to take care of him. To help him. But I have to respect his wishes."

She sighed. "He is stubborn."

He gave a wry nod.

They sat for a long time, quietly, just watching Gabby as he slept off his drunken state. Every once in a while, he would moan and thrash, and Kaiya would settle a hand on his brow to calm him. As the night wore on and she watched Gabby sleep, her mind turned once more to Cipher's enigma and the question of whether he'd deliberately used the locker numbers as a type of legend. If he did, perhaps it was a key to solving Cipher's damn code.

"What was Cipher's real name?" she asked with her hands.

"Brian."

She grimaced. There went that theory.

"Why?"

"I thought maybe he used the lockers as a nod to his name. Or an anagram, and if so, they might be a way to unravel his code."

"Good theory. That would be…" He started counting on his fingers. "JZF. Right?"

"Yes," she signed.

"Any other ideas?"

She shook her head. Her conversation with Lisa drifted through her mind. Should she bring up the way the other woman seemed to be drilling for answers?

"When are we leaving the Whiskey Knights?" she asked in sign.

"As soon as we all get up and move around," he said. "Why?"

"I don't trust these people."

"You aren't alone in that regard."

They lapsed back into silence, and the night stretched on. Every now and again, Gabby would twitch, and she'd soothe back his hair until he quieted. Seeing him so vulnerable hurt her heart. For so long, she'd silently screamed the question, "*Why me?*" Why had it been *her* hearing that had been taken away? Why had *she* been the one punished when she'd been such a good girl? How was going deaf at ten fair? Yet, as she stared at Gabby, she'd finally gotten her answers.

Because she was selfish.

She'd whined and cursed the fates that had taken away her hearing and had given her a family that had locked her away. Yet never once in her whole life, had she considered some people had it worse. Even knowing Chloe's horrible background, all Kaiya had seen was the fact that her cousin was free to live her own life. To enjoy the intimate nature of sounds around her. Kaiya had been jealous of a woman who'd killed her own mother and had been sent to a psychiatric home as a teenager. It made Kaiya pathetic and ungrateful. So why not take away her hearing?

Gabby had suffered and suffered still, much like Chloe had. Shame sliced through Kaiya, making her stomach queasy. Her character revelation painted a horrible picture, and she resolved to find whatever help Gabby needed to heal him of his tormented past. To free him from the shackles that chained him to a bed every night in order to ensure he never hurt another innocent person.

Perhaps having her hearing taken away had been the only way for her to become a more compassionate human being. Coming to terms with that consumed her for the rest of the night.

Chapter Fifteen

Sunlight tickled her eyelids. Kaiya roused and a sharp crick in her neck had her wincing. She sat up from her slumped-over position on the bed and saw that Gabby watched her with flat, emotionless eyes. She rolled her shoulders as she smiled at him, but he didn't return the gesture.

"Are you okay?" she signed.

He looked away from her and moved his arms. Boone walked in from the bathroom, a towel around his waist, and proceeded to unlock the cuffs. Gabby sat up and rubbed them before untying his ankles. He handed the paraphernalia back to Boone, who tucked it away in his saddlebag once more.

All of this done without one glance in her direction. Kaiya's heart ached.

"You let her sleep next to me?"

Gabby addressed his question to Boone, but she read his lips and grabbed his hand. Finally, he looked at her with cold, hard eyes.

"I wanted to take care of you," she signed.

"Don't do it again," he said, pulling away.

"Why?"

"Because I'm dangerous."

She shook her head. "You should get some help."

"I'm doing fine. I don't *need* some shrink thinking they can get in my head to figure me out. No one can know what the fuck is going on in here." He tapped his temple.

"I messed up before, with what I said about you not understanding what it felt like about being in a cage," she said with her hands. "I don't know your story, but I see the ending. You cannot keep this bottled up. It will eat you alive. If you don't want a psychologist then talk to me."

"I don't want your pity."

For a moment, she wondered how she could convince him that the last thing she felt was pity, then it dawned on her that she and Gabby were very similar. She might be selfish, but she, too, had dealt with her own issue of insecurity as best as she could. Kaiya took a deep, steadying breath.

"I…do not…pity you," she said aloud. The vibrations of the words reverberated through her body, but it terrified her because she had no idea how she sounded. Would he be repulsed? She flicked a gaze at Boone. Would they leave her in disgust because she sounded stupid? "I understand."

He let go of her hand, and she closed her eyes, breathing hard as her heart raced. She'd been prevented from actually living for so long she'd forgotten the terror of what it felt like to be rejected. For a brief moment in time, she'd been happy, living in a make-believe world where the two men she cared about could possibly love her back. Her grandfather had placed her in a cage, but Gabby and Boone had set her free in the only way she could be free. They had given her a single moment of happiness.

Gabby slid his big, warm hand under her chin to cup her face and tilt her head up. He looked deep into her eyes. "You talked to me."

She nodded, her heart thudding so heavily in her chest she was afraid of having heart failure. The coldness melted away to reveal the tenderness of his smile. Her stomach flipped over.

"Not out of pity," he stated.

She shook her head. No, she'd never pity him, no matter his story. The rage drained from him, and his shoulders drooped.

"We were prisoners of war," he said, staring directly at her so she could read his lips as well as the emotions flittering over his face. "Young kids back then, although we thought we were all grown up. I was big, even then, the biggest in my platoon, so it gave the insurgents the great idea of pitting me against fellow soldiers. Bloody battles I wanted no part of. I didn't want to fight them, but when they shot a few in front of me, well, I figured a few bruises were better than being dead."

Kaiya's breath hitched in her chest. Gabby's eyes were flat, emotionless.

"Eventually, they got tired of the sport." He took a deep breath. "An air raid took out one of their camps. They were beyond pissed. Decided their point could be made better with a bunch of dead soldiers than live ones."

Her gaze darted toward Boone, but his was fixed into space, as if he were reliving that time as Gabby told the story. She took hold of Gabby's hand.

"They had captured two reporters," he said. "Young, stupid college graduates trying to make a name for themselves. They had no business being in that country. Being on the front lines." He swallowed thickly. "The insurgents put us on a firing line. I… We were going to die, so I had nothing to lose."

"What did you do?" she asked, remembering how to form her mouth for the words.

"I charged the guards. They fought back." He touched the scar on his face. "Eventually, I got hold of a gun and I killed most of them before someone threw a grenade. It landed near Boone."

Boone stepped forward. "He tackled me. Protected me. The grenade went off and Gabby got the brunt of the impact. Destroyed his hearing."

Gabby gave her a wry smile. "Worked out, I suppose. For a while, I thought I had lost hearing in both ears, so I learned sign language. Eventually, the swelling went down and I got one ear back."

Kaiya raised a hand and brushed her fingers down the scar on his face then over to his bad ear. He shied away, but she wouldn't let him pull too far back. She didn't want him to hide who he was anymore. For a long while, he held her. No sexual overtures, no heavy emotions. He simply drew strength from her body, and she freely gave it. Gradually, the hand on her lower back traveled downward until he gripped an ass cheek. He ground his pelvis into hers, and his hard cock pushed into her soft belly.

Kaiya took the initiative and kissed him, claiming his lips passionately and not letting him retreat any farther. She demanded his submission, and he stiffened against her. She knew he knew she wanted his surrender—to her, to this relationship, to who he really was. A moment later, he gave it, although he turned the tables on her and swept her up in a tight embrace.

He laid her on the bed and loomed over her, tasting of the bitter swill of whiskey from the night before. It should have grossed her out, but it didn't, and his frenetic need for her wiped everything else away. The side of the bed dipped as Boone joined them, and she broke the kiss on a gasp to turn toward him. He'd only been wearing a towel and untied it to let his cock spring forward. She reached for his dick, and he thrust his hips forward to allow her to swallow him down. She knew this wasn't going to be slow lovemaking, or even romantic. Gabby's reaction—hell, her *own* desire—simmered too close to the top. It was always like this between them, though. Last night her body had gone up in flames for Boone, but today, Gabby revved her engine.

Gabby pulled at her shirt, and she helped him as much as possible without breaking her lip lock around Boone's cock. Impatiently, he pushed her T-shirt up around her neck and ripped apart her bra. He cupped her breasts, filling his palms with their slight weight and teasing the nipples all over again. She thrust her chest out, wanting more, and Gabby leaned over her, nipping and licking all the way down, until he knelt between her thighs. He unzipped her pants and pulled them down, exposing her inch by inch to his gaze. Boone spread his fingers into her hair to keep her still while he fucked her face with his dick, but that didn't stop Gabby from wanting to eat her pussy. Like her bra, he tore off her thong and went down on her. He licked his way up and down her slit, over and over, until she thought she would go out of her mind. Her juices flowed, and he lapped them up, taking his sweet old time. Then he found the spot that cried for attention, the little bundle of nerves hidden within a hood, and sucked it into the hot vortex of his mouth while he pressed his fingers inward.

He bent one finger, rubbing along the back wall of her pussy while he continued to suck on her clit. White-hot fire roared through her as she went up in flames. She gasped around the big cock in her mouth, and a shudder tore through Boone's body. Abruptly, both men pulled away, and she was left lying spread eagle feeling empty and bereft until Boone hauled her up onto her hands and knees. Now, she had Gabby's big dick in her face and Boone caressing the globes of her ass.

Boone spread her legs wide and kissed her inner thighs, working his way up until he latched onto her pussy from behind. She arched in pleasure as he swept his tongue into her channel to lick up and down. He found her clit and rubbed it gently in circles, and just when she thought it couldn't feel any better, he withdrew his mouth. Before she realized what he was doing, he found her rosette and began to lick around the puckered sphincter. A riot of feelings burst within her, embarrassment at first soon gave way to pleasure, and she was unprepared for the way her body surged with desire. Moving close behind her, he ran a single finger around her asshole. The movement tickled, but felt deliciously sordid, and when he pushed his finger inward, Kaiya relaxed enough to allow entry. The intrusion made her whole body shudder, then Gabby was probing her mouth with the tip of his cock, taking her mind away from what Boone was doing. She opened her lips and Gabby surged in, immediately setting up a rhythm. She clamped her lips around the shaft and hollowed out her cheeks.

Then Boone withdrew, and something wet and cold dripped over her anus. Lube, she realized a second before the blunt tip of Boone's cockhead pressed against her. She did her best to relax, remembering all the stuff she'd read about the backdoor breech, as well as the porn she loved to watch. Nothing prepared her for the assault, however, and that's exactly how it felt for a few good minutes as Boone seesawed his way in. Although he did take it slowly and carefully, giving only an inch before backing out, it still burned like hell each time he slid forward.

Breathing deeply through her nose, Kaiya had just reached the conclusion that she didn't much care for anal sex, until Boone suddenly decided to drive hard, sinking his substantial cock right up to the hilt. She gasped, and tears rose to her eyes. A burning pain shot through her, but the discomfort was accompanied by the most exquisite sensation of fullness and friction she'd ever felt in her life. Boone held her hips, swiveled, and suddenly pleasure flushed over her whole body. She gasped as he found her clit with his fingers, stroking it vigorously while his dick caressed the inside of her back passage.

Why the hell have I not tried this before?

Pain and pleasure sent her head spinning. She sucked the cock in her mouth harder, and Gabby suddenly pulled out of her mouth. He grabbed his dick, pumped and sprayed all over her tits that bounced with the force of Boone pumping into her ass. Hot cum covered her chest, dripped off her pebbled nipples. A huge wave of sexual electricity unleashed through her whole body, and she came so hard stars bloomed behind her eyes. Clutching her hips in a vise-like grip, Boone ejaculated deep inside her ass.

After a moment, he pulled out and fell onto the bed, dragging her down to his side. She was sweating, panting, and covered in cum — and loved every sticky inch of it. Gabby crawled on the bed and flopped onto his back. She smoothed a hand over the hairs on his chest and traced the tattoos decorating his flesh. He turned his head and they stared at each another.

"You are the strongest man I know," she said.

But he only looked away, avoiding her gaze, and unease unfurled within her as if a ghost had just walked across her grave.

Chapter Sixteen

"Are they there now?"

Lisa stared down from the bedroom window at the two men, Gabby and Boone, and the woman, Kaiya. She honestly didn't know what the two big handsome men saw in that skinny bitch. Sure, she looked hot when she'd climaxed last night, but the girl was weak. Anyone could see that. Two men like Gabby and Boone needed someone tough enough to be an old lady, able to handle all the bitches who threw their pussies at them in hopes they'd be the ones to take the place in their beds. There'd been many cunts she'd had to beat the shit out of in order to hold onto Stone Cold. He may be old as fuck, but he was the president and damned if she would let him go until she was ready.

"Yes," she said, answering her lover's question. "I'm staring at them right now. They're securing their saddlebags, getting ready to head toward Sioux City."

"And Stone Cold is friendly with them?"

"He is and he isn't," she said dismissively. "You know any angle he can find, he's going to exploit."

"Yeah. He tried working that angle on me."

"Is that why you left so suddenly?"

"You know why I left," he said quietly.

"Yes," she replied. "Although I didn't like you leaving me."

"I had to." He sighed. "There wasn't room for me with the Whiskey Knights. What can you tell me about them?"

Lisa snapped her attention back to the three visitors getting readying themselves to leave. "The bitch is deaf."

"You sure?"

"Positive. Sign language and everything."

"Well, that makes her slightly more interesting."

"Hey, now," Lisa snapped. She'd invested too much time and energy for her lover to have interest in some other cunt. "I'll end the bitch right now."

"Don't be jealous. I simply meant she's not that much of a looker, so now I understand what makes those two assholes want to protect her."

"She is quite homely," Lisa replied, sniffing disdainfully. "No tits, no ass."

"I'm sure she lies there and fucks like a board."

She chuckled. "No doubt. So when am I supposed to meet up with you? This waiting around is annoying."

Lisa tapped her nails against the ledge as the inertia of biding her time surged inside her like an insidious vine, strangling her. Every day she remained was one more night of fucking the old man.

"I'll let you know. Right now, I need them to get that fucking locker open. The promise of money can't be overlooked."

"I know. I want the fucking money. Why don't you just force it open?" she asked. "Are you an outlaw or aren't you?"

"Don't fucking insult me, Lisa."

146

"I'm sorry, baby, but I have to put up with that old cock fucking me every night."

"You don't have to stay with him, you know. You're a smart woman. A *gifted* woman."

She sighed. "And I'm all yours. I miss you."

"Miss you too, sweetheart. But we're almost home free, ready to fly away with our investment to live like kings."

"So get the locker open now," she whined.

"The bus depot is in the decent part of the fucking town. The police station is across the street. Besides, there needs to be a reckoning with those two goddamn assholes. They took away something important to me, something I loved, so I'm going to fucking take from them."

Lisa eyed Kaiya again as Boone ran a loving finger down her cheek. Hateful jealousy tore through her. She wanted what the deaf girl had. Her lover might not be as handsome as Boone, but at least he'd eventually have the cash to keep her in love with him. "The girl."

"She's one thing. Maybe the main thing. An eye for an eye. Is she fucking them both?"

"I don't know," Lisa admitted. "She's only been with Boone as far as I can tell."

"That's good enough for me. It's time that man learns what it feels like to lose something he loves."

"Then we'll be together?"

"Yes, sweetheart. I'll text you when to meet me so we can get the fuck out of here."

"With the cash, right?" she demanded. Otherwise, she wasn't going anywhere without the security of liquid cash flow.

"Don't worry. You'll be swimming in more money than you know what to do with for the rest of your life."

Lisa smiled at the promise in his voice. Being an old lady—the *head* old lady—certainly had its perks, but the thought of a younger dick and more money than she knew what to do with had her pussy wet with longing. Stone Cold walked up to Boone ready, no doubt, to say goodbye. She flicked a dismissive glance over the old man from head to toe as she disconnected the call. A girl could only stand so much shriveled cock in her lifetime.

* * * *

"I suppose I should thank you for your hospitality," Boone said to Stone Cold as he secured the saddlebags in preparation for their ride to Sioux City.

"It's generally the polite thing to do."

Boone snorted. "I'm not a very polite man. And you basically railroaded us."

Stone Cold shrugged. "You say tomato, I say toe-mah-toe."

"The ending of that little song is let's call the whole thing off," Boone said. He held Stone Cold's gaze until the other man chuckled.

"You never give an inch, do you?"

"No," Boone replied. "Like I said, I'll talk to Romeo for a sit down, but I won't guarantee anything."

Stone Cold held out his hand, and Boone hesitated in taking it. The feeling that something else was going on hit him again, and the questions that plagued him earlier returned in full force. He grabbed the man's hand and pulled him close to murmur in his ear.

"How did you know so much about the Men of Hell?"

Stone Cold jerked back, and their gazes clashed—held. A power play erupted but Boone refused to back down. This wasn't his president or his club, and he didn't give a shit about protocol.

"Watch who you're talking to, boy."

"Old men like you must be getting senile if you think I give a fuck about who you are," Boone taunted. He glanced around at the Whiskey Knights who eyed him coldly, ready to jump in and defend their leader if need be. "My club was under attack from one of your men. If you want to stick to the law of the land, then you know I have the right to retribution."

Stone Cold clenched his jaw so tightly Boone wondered how he didn't crack it. He tried to apply pressure to the handshake, but Boone gave an equal amount, if not more so. No way was Boone backing down from this asshole.

"I told you Vicious went rogue. You're going to need my help in wrangling him."

Boone sneered and squeezed the fingers hard enough to see a slight wince on the other man's face before he let go.

Stone Cold flexed his hand. "Vicious called me last night," he said. "Drunk, babbling about how he'd found the mother lode. How he was going to bring your club down if it was the last thing he did. Now, I wasn't lying when I said I'd like a business arrangement with the Men of Hell, and seeing my future business partners die because of one of my men doesn't sit right with me, even if he was voted out."

"So you want to help out of the generosity of your heart? I don't think so. What else?"

Stone Cold's gaze darted to the duffel Gabby was currently stuffing into his saddlebag.

Boone snorted derisively. "So you want a slice of what's inside."

"No," Stone Cold said. "Vicious said a mother lode. You think I'm too foolish not to realize that a hundred grand has to be the tip of the iceberg?"

"You know *nothing*," Boone stressed.

Stone Cold grabbed Boone's upper arm. "I could kill you easily and simply take the money."

"Is that the immediate answer of the Whiskey Knights?" Gabby asked. His hand hovered over the butt of his gun. "Simply take what you can't have? You sure seem to have bred that into your men."

Boone held up a hand to hold him back.

"On second thought, the Men of Hell aren't for sale. Thanks for your hospitality but don't bother waiting for a phone call."

He broke the grip on his arm and moved toward his bike.

"Don't be a fool! Our clubs could rule Nebraska."

Boone straddled his bike and saw out of the corner of his eye that Gabby had done the same thing. Kaiya wrapped her arms around him as he glared at Stone Cold.

"If ruling Nebraska means ruling it with the Knights, I think I'll pass," he said coldly.

He made a come-along gesture with his fingers to Gabby then punched his bike into gear. They roared down the road without looking back.

Chapter Seventeen

They crossed into South Dakota and wasted no time in making a beeline for the Sioux City Downtown Bus Depot. The key to the last locker burned a hole in Kaiya's pocket and she couldn't wait to put this scavenger hunt behind her. If there was one thing she'd learned on this trip, it was that she was in love — with both Gabby and Boone. When she'd first learned about Chloe's relationship with Dax and Romeo, it had surprised her. Sure, Chloe had always been a bit wild. Killing one's mother tended to make a person go off the deep end. But she'd found a semblance of calmness being with the Men of Hell, and Kaiya longed for the same thing. Her problems were nowhere near the level that Chloe had dealt with, obviously, but that didn't diminish her own need for a place to belong.

Her ass was getting used to the vibration of the motorcycle. She tightened her arms around Boone, hugging him, and was rewarded with a pat on her hand. She glanced over her shoulder and saw Gabby cruising along, goggles covering his face and the long strands of his hair whipping under the edge of his helmet. He smiled and gave her a wave. Excitement flared to life within her. Once they got the money from the locker, she had a vision of them spending the rest of the day in bed together, all three of them living out one of her deepest fantasies. She wanted to be owned and possessed by both of them, at the same time. Taken in one of the most primitive and raw ways a woman could be taken. The thoughts sent a jolt of pleasure directly to her center and she clenched her pussy in a mock Kegel imitation. It didn't ease the desire flooding through her and the bike's pulsing between her thighs wasn't helping her sexual high at all.

All too soon, however, they were on the streets of Sioux City, and this time the bus depot was located in a nice area of the city. New and modern, with clean lines and sleek angles, it lacked the seedier quality of the two other stations they'd been to.

Boone and Gabby filed into parking spots and shut off their bikes. Kaiya dismounted and took off her helmet as the men did the same. The sun shone warmly on her skin. The cerulean tint of the sky held big fluffy clouds that lazily drifted by. Gabby tapped Boone's arm and pointed, and when she followed the line, she saw they were directly across the street from a police station.

"Vicious wouldn't dare strike with the cops right there," she signed. "This should be a piece of cake."

"Don't get too comfortable," Gabby signed back. "Believe me, Vicious and Cipher won't let the police get in their way. And this is the last step in finding us."

She shook her head. "You're being paranoid. This place is so peaceful."

She held her arms open and half twirled as she lifted her face to the sky. She breathed in the fresh air and turned to smile at her men. They both stared at her skeptically.

"Let me get the bag," she signed. The faster she got it, the faster they could get to a hotel.

But Gabby held her arm and shook his head. "This time we get the bag."

"Why?" she asked with her fingers. "I thought you'd want to keep a lookout."

"The last time you went inside, Eagle found you," he said.

She read his lips and frowned. "You cannot compare this situation to Omaha. There are no Whiskey Knights around here. Come on. I will be in and out in five minutes."

Gabby glanced at Boone, who shrugged.

Kaiya smiled, stood on tiptoe and kissed Gabby's cheek before dashing up the steps to the depot's entrance. Large skylights allowed massive amounts of sunlight into the station. Lush, green plants decorated the lobby, next to nice vinyl seats and large television screens playing various soap operas and news reports. The lockers were located on the opposite side of the check-in counter, and she headed in that direction. The faceplates were bright orange, and she traced the numbers until she came to number ten. Digging the key out of her pocket, she quickly unlocked it and opened the door to grab the duffel that waited, only there was one other thing inside the small compartment. Draping the bag's strap over her shoulder, she picked the object up and realized it was a book. Or specifically, a journal. Her heart thudded with excitement as she flipped through it and noticed it was full of handwritten notes. A ledger. Perhaps the missing ledger she needed to connect all of Cipher's dots?

Kaiya flung her own backpack off her shoulders to stuff the journal inside just as a hand grabbed her arm and a gun barrel pressed against her ribs. She stiffened, knowing without looking who held her captive. He yanked on her arm and, helplessly, she followed.

A moment later, the entire place lit up as fire ripped through the serene interior of the bus depot, completely shattering the tranquil setting.

* * * *

Gabby watched her leave, his gaze focused on her sexy ass. Emotion swelled inside him, yet he hesitated calling it love. Who was he to know what love actually was? Besides, he was the last man on Earth who was worthy of anything as monumental as that feeling. He wasn't even worthy of being in Kaiya's shadow, let alone thinking of a happily ever after with her. Still, he didn't think he could let her go. Not now. Even though she deserved better.

The club…he understood that life. It suited him. When he'd come home from the military hospital, he'd been a mess. Homeless. Wandering. There was no way he could've functioned normally in society back then, and a few years later, Boone had come to find him. If it hadn't been for the club, he would have been lost in the darkness.

"Stop it," Boone ordered.

Gabby tore his gaze off Kaiya's lush ass to look at him. "Stop what?"

"You don't think I don't know that look?" Boone asked, pointing at his face.

"What look?" Gabby scoffed.

"Don't go back to that place, Gordon Dixon. You are not that man anymore. Hear me?"

"Shut the fuck up," Gabby said sharply.

"I will never shut up about this," Boone said.

Gabby turned away and reached for the crumpled pack of cigarettes in his pocket, trying to convey without words that he was done with the conversation.

After a pause, Boone sighed. "So after this we have a meeting with Red Eye."

"Yep."

"Figured we'd rest up today, head out tomorrow."

"Fine."

"Jesus," Boone muttered. "I fucking hate it when you get moody."

At that moment, the world simply shattered as an explosion rocked the ground, emanating from the station. The acrid smell of gunpowder permeated the air as glass rained down. Gabby and Boone were blown back and fell into their bikes, which toppled over from the force of their bodies. Car alarms shrieked through the unnatural calmness that suddenly descended. Gabby shook his head, trying to get his bearings, and looked at Boone to make sure he was okay, then he whipped his head around to the bus depot. Panic descended into his heart as fire licked from the windows.

"Kaiya," he whispered brokenly.

He and Boone both pushed to their feet and ran to the entrance. By this time, the shock of what had happened turned into horror and people from all around began to rush forward to help. Cops poured out of the police station.

"Kaiya!" Boone bellowed. But, of course, she wouldn't be able to hear him.

Sirens wailed in the distance, quickly coming closer. Victims stumbled out of the front of the station, disoriented, streaked in soot and blood. Gabby and

Boone tried pressing forward but the swarm of bodies made it difficult, and when they finally made it inside, Gabby's stomach bottomed out. Smoke hung thickly through the air, constricting his breathing. He coughed and raised his arm to cover his face as his eyes watered from the lingering heat. Even though debris and soot lined everything, a blackened explosion pattern ran next to the main window, which had been the glass that had shattered all over them. Two bodies lay in pieces next to the destruction, and Boone clutched his shoulder, pointing. Gabby swung around and saw the lockers, which hadn't been damaged. They hurried over, dodging debris, to find Kaiya. Only she wasn't there.

Firemen poured into the scene.

"Out! Out! Everyone, out!"

A few moans came forth, and some firemen moved toward the sounds. Another man grabbed Gabby's arm.

"You have to get out now!"

"Fuck!" Gabby yelled. "Kaiya! Where are you!"

"Sir, you have to leave!"

Gabby pulled away. "Kaiya! Kaiya!"

"Sir…"

Gabby ducked away from the firefighter, turned and shoved him back. "I'm not leaving here without my girlfriend! Kaiya!"

He stomped forward until he found locker number ten. Seeing the key in place let them know that it was empty. The merchandise inside was gone. He glanced toward the victims still inside and studied their faces. She wasn't among them.

"Maybe she made it out before the bomb went off," Gabby said. He looked up at Boone. "Maybe we missed her coming out."

"Maybe," Boone said, although his tone implied that he doubted it.

"You have to leave!"

The fireman was persistent, Gabby would give him that. "Yeah, yeah," he said. "We're going."

He needed to hold onto the hope she hadn't been inside when the place exploded, but it was as if she'd simply vanished. They hurried out of the interior and bent over at the waist, coughing up a lungful of black residual smoke. Gabby stared at each victim, looking for Kaiya, but she wasn't among them either.

"He was waiting for us after all," Boone said.

Gabby tore his gaze from searching the battered and bruised people. Boone's fists were clenched so tightly the whites of his knuckles stood out in stark relief.

"You mean Vicious," Gabby clarified. It wasn't a question.

"Stone Cold said I would need his help. Fuck!" Boone yelled, breathing hard. He pulled his cell phone out of his pocket and punched in a number. As the call went through, Boone captured his gaze. "We find that motherfucker and tear his fucking heart out."

It was a burning pledge, one that Gabby felt in his own soul.

Chapter Eighteen

Although Kaiya couldn't hear what was going on, she saw the devastation raining around them just as Vicious shoved her into an old van. He'd dragged her quickly outside a moment before the building seemed to explode, and her heart nearly burst from fear. Had Gabby and Boone stayed outside? She hoped to God they had, because if they'd been inside…if *anything* had happened to them… It made her heart ache painfully.

Cipher's gleeful face suddenly popped in her line of vision, and Kaiya vowed to kill either or both bastards the first chance she got.

"Give me the journal," Cipher demanded.

She read his lips, but she stubbornly refused to acknowledge him.

He grabbed her jaw between his fingers and applied enough pressure to make her squirm in pain.

"The journal, bitch!"

She couldn't control how her gaze flickered to the backpack she clutched, and he followed her eye movement. He let her go, pushing her back to grab it up and open it. She watched in fury as he pulled out the leather-bound book and skimmed through it. From his pocket, he withdrew a square device and it took her a moment to figure out it was a GPS locator.

Vicious got into the van and started it up.

She looked helplessly out of the passenger mirror and watched the bus depot getting farther behind. Almost immediately, they were lost in the sea of fire trucks and ambulances arriving, along with people hurrying forward either to help the bombing victims or just to get a thrill from everyone's suffering. She wanted to weep for those who had been caught in Vicious' debauchery. She'd seen the euphoric pleasure plastered on his face that he'd taken in hurting all the innocent people, poor souls who happened to be at the wrong place at the wrong time. Why hadn't she taken Boone's warning more seriously?

She stared at Cipher, consumed with hate, as he ignored her to focus on the journal in his hands. He simply didn't give a shit that so many had been wounded, possibly killed, by his actions. How could this piece of shit have been part of the Men of Hell? Sure, they were no angels, but they didn't destroy innocent bystanders just for the hell of it. And her club didn't betray one another. She didn't even blink at the thought that she claimed the Men of Hell as her own. She had come in as an outsider, a promise made by Chloe, and reluctantly agreed to by Romeo, but Kaiya stood firm by Gabby's and Boone's sides, and she'd do anything to protect them. Kaiya took a deep breath and embraced the knowledge that what she would have to do to survive might be soul altering, but she wouldn't hesitate to do what she had to for herself and her men — or for the club.

"You're going to die today," she signed to Cipher.

Her hand movements must have caught his eye because he looked at her. "I can't read sign language."

She knew that. That didn't stop her from continuing. "I'm going to kill you, Cipher. For me. For those people who you just hurt. For the Men of Hell. I'll find some way to kill you."

Kaiya stared at him in the eye, trying to convey all the hate she was feeling. Slowly, she smirked at him. Cipher's nostrils flared with his anger and before she knew what he planned, he backhanded her. Stars exploded through her head just before darkness descended.

* * * *

"You called," Stone Cold said mockingly as soon as he picked up the call.

"Turn on your fucking news," Boone ground out as he began walking away from the chaos all around them. Gabby followed on his heels. Boone glanced at their bikes, laying on their sides like beached whales. There were too many people around to dig them out of the rubble. He began looking around for an alternative method to get the hell out of there.

"What's that noise?"

"Your little psycho blew up the bus depot in Sioux City," he replied. "He took Kaiya."

There was a short pause. "Are you sure?"

"Of course I'm fucking sure! Now, you're going to tell me where he is."

"How the hell would I know that?" Stone Cold demanded.

"Because you told me I was going to need your help. You told me he called you. You've been playing me from day one, you piece of lying shit." He broke off and took a deep breath, closing his eyes on a fucking prayer. "Please. He has my woman."

There was some rustling around in the background, as if Stone Cold were moving it around. A muffled voice swam through the connection, then Stone Cold cleared his throat. "Eagle thinks he may know where they're heading."

Boone's heart jumped in hope. "Where?"

"There's a small town back in Nebraska, off the 77, called Highwinds. He's probably headed there."

"Why?" Boone demanded. "What's there?"

"It belongs to the Knights."

"What? The whole town?"

Stone Cold sighed. "It's more like a farm. We store things there, although it's not easy to get to."

Something about his tone didn't ring true. "Are you fucking with me? You send me to some made up fucking place so you can get to him and the fucking cash he has first? If anything happens to Kaiya, I will personally hunt you down and empty my clip in your forehead."

"Listen, I obviously don't know what he's thinking, but if he needs to lie low, he'll be there."

Boone locked gazes with Gabby. What was he supposed to do? Trust the one man he couldn't trust at all? "You said off the 77?"

"Yeah. Down a road called John Zinger Field."

Everything inside Boone tightened. The conversation he had with Kaiya about the locker numbers rolled through his head. "That's where she's at."

"Now you sound sure about it."

"I am," he said grimly and hung up. He nodded to their bikes. "We need to get our wheels."

Gabby cracked his knuckles and turned away. "Already on it."

Chapter Nineteen

"I'm going to fuck her in the ass, then I'm going to blow her apart, bullet by bullet," Vicious suddenly said out of the blue.

He'd been thinking about what to do to the deaf girl for the hour he'd been driving. In his mind, he pictured every single filthy thing he could do to Boone's bitch. It had been a complete tossup on who was going to be their prisoner, because the way Vicious figured it, any of them would've been a good candidate for revenge. Boone to flat out torture and kill, his big mute of a sidekick, or the deaf pussy that road behind him. It just so happened that he got the girl.

"What?" Cipher said distractedly.

"I'm going to fuck her in the ass," Vicious repeated. "Then I'll blow out her kneecaps, her pelvis, hands. Break her collarbone. She'll be a bloody stain on the floor when Boone finally finds her."

Cipher stared at him, his mouth forming a little circle of disbelief. "You can't do that to her."

"Why the fuck not?" Vicious demanded.

"I may do a lot of shit, but I don't rape women."

Vicious shrugged. "You won't be raping her. I will."

In his head, he played through the scenario and how satisfying a tribute it will be to honor Bizerk's memory. He didn't even have Bizerk's body, having left it behind as he'd fled. There wouldn't be a tomb or monument dedicated to Bizerk, so the girl would have to do. A sacrifice to appease the ghost haunting him.

"She hasn't done anything to you," Cipher stressed.

"Shut up!" Vicious snarled. "Her association with the Men of Hell is all I need to condemn her. If she suffers, then Boone suffers."

He didn't add afterward that he would kill Cipher, take all his stash and bury the man in the woods, never to be found again. No one would miss the nerdy accountant, and he'd take the fucking money and go after the Whiskey Knights next. The club was supposed to have his back, be his Brothers, but Stone Cold was only interested in the club's bottom line. Stone Cold had turned his back on him, so they'd be the next to fall. Then he'd create a club dynasty that would send all men cowering in fear. He could almost hear his future brothers chanting his name. Perhaps he'd name his club after his fallen love.

The rest of the trip was spent in silence. He didn't care. Cipher was simply a means to an end and once Vicious had what he wanted, that would be all he needed of the man. He'd first approached the man in hopes of ferreting out any information on Boone and Gabby, but once he had learned there was a shit load of money involved, Cipher's fate had been sealed.

"Turn there," Cipher said, pointing to a road that was mostly hidden by the woods.

"I know how to get to Highwinds," Vicious snapped.

"John Zinger Field. I buried the money off this road."

"You buried money? Are you a fucking idiot?"

"What?" Cipher demanded. "I stole a shit load of money from the Master and the Men of Hell. I had to hide it and I didn't want to put it all in one place in case it was ever discovered."

"So you gave yourself a fucking treasure map?" Vicious snorted derisively. "I bet your favorite book growing up was *Treasure Island*."

"Shut up," Cipher said coldly. "And drive one point five miles."

"Whatever," Vicious muttered.

He drove. Hell, whatever mother lode bullshit Cipher spouted about was worth putting up with the little dick for a tad longer. And once he had whatever Cipher had buried, well, no one would miss him in these thick woods.

"Here," Cipher said. "I remember this area now."

Vicious pulled over and turned off the engine. As he got out of the van, he heard Cipher waking up the cunt. She moaned and the breathless little whimper of pain made his dick harden. Perhaps it wouldn't be such a chore after all to fuck the whore.

The back of the van opened, and Cipher jumped out before turning to pull the reluctant woman with him. He smirked at her and all she did was lift her chin, as if she were too good for him. Fucking bitch. Soon, he'd show her just how low she actually was.

"Come on," he said. "Let's get your fucking treasure."

He clamped a hand on her wrist and led her forward. Cipher hurried to lead the way, holding up his compass and journal as they traveled deeper into the woods.

* * * *

"She better not be fucking dead," Gabby muttered as they pushed through the dense underbrush.

"Don't say that," Boone ordered.

"Are you sure we're going the right way?" Gabby asked.

Boone pointed to a rag tied to a tree. "Stone Cold said this was the shortcut."

"Why couldn't we just take a fucking road?"

"No road."

Gabby grunted. "If this place is their holding warehouse then there's a fucking road *somewhere*. He's fucking with us."

"Maybe."

"Bullshit," Gabby muttered.

Boone spun and grabbed his cut, yanking him close. "What would you have me do? Huh? This is all I have to go on!"

Gabby brought his arms up and through Boone's to break the hold. "They were *hunting* us, Boone!"

"I know!" Boone yelled. He flexed his jaw, as if gritting his teeth together. "Don't you think I know they were watching our every fucking move? That attack in Lincoln was them playing with us. It was why they never showed up in Omaha! They realized we were following the key trail and they laid in wait."

"Then why the hell didn't we see it?" Gabby raged. "So fucking obvious." He turned and kicked a tree stump in anger and frustration. He flashed back to that fateful day, as he'd stood tied up next to the insurgent who had led him forward to be killed. They were all to die by firing squad. He was first, the two reporters were next and Boone was last. They were to serve as a warning for any and all to get the hell out of their country.

"I didn't see the consequences of my actions that day either," Gabby whispered. "I didn't mean to get those two reporters killed."

Boone froze, staring at him. Gabby knew he was shocked. Hell, this was a subject he had personally declared off limits, and to bring it up now, in possibly the worst moment ever, was way out of character.

"Gabby—"

"I knew we were all going to die, so I just reacted."

"You did the right thing."

Gabby shook his head. "You say that because you're still here. But those two young men are gone because I acted foolishly."

"You acted *bravely*."

Gabby snorted. "No, Boone. I was a coward. I didn't want to die, especially trussed up like a turkey awaiting slaughter. I joined the military because I had no choice, not because I wanted to die for some damned glorified concept." He ran a shaking hand through his hair as tears filled his eyes. "It was all a joke... One big damn joke for me. But not to you. And not to the men of our platoon. Not to those reporters. And because I was selfish, they died."

Boone grabbed his jacket and hauled him close. They stared at each another.

"Listen to me. It doesn't matter how or why you were there. We were all dead that day, but the difference you made was that their bodies weren't desecrated. They were brought home to their families. There are two mothers who won't ever have to wonder what happened to their sons because you made sure our deaths wouldn't go unknown, or unavenged. You took a fucking grenade for me, Gordon. If you were truly selfish, you wouldn't have risked your life like that."

For the first time in his adult life, tears poured down Gabby's cheeks. They may have been silent, but he cried for the men he didn't save that day as well as for the grief and self-loathing he had harbored for years. Boone pulled him in tight and anchored him to the ground. Otherwise, he thought he might float up and away as each layer of guilt was stripped away. When the tide had run its course, his shoulders felt lighter. The bleeding dam in his heart had been plugged. He wasn't completely whole, but the first step toward self-forgiveness had been breached.

"Gabby?" Boone asked.

Gabby looked at his friend. He hadn't known Boone that well, even though they'd been through boot camp together and stationed in the same unit. But now the man was his best friend and he was thankful to have him in his life.

"I'm good," he said and wiped his eyes.

"I wouldn't use that particular adjective."

Gabby snorted. "No. I suppose not. I mean, thank you. For all you've done for me."

Boone smiled. "You saved my life, Brother. The least I could do was return the favor. Now, let's go get our girl."

"Yeah." Our girl. He liked the sound of that.

At that moment, a gunshot rang out through the woods. They turned. The sound had been faint and had pinged from the west.

"We're too far away," Gabby muttered.

"Come on," Boone replied. They ran as fast as possible through the thick underbrush.

They hadn't gone too far when the second gunshot echoed around them — closer.

"I hope to fucking God that was Kaiya killing both of those assholes," Gabby said.

"Me too," Boone replied grimly.

Chapter Twenty

"She's deaf," Cipher said.

They both faced her, with Vicious maliciously staring at her. She was able to follow along with their heated debate.

"You don't have to hurt her, Vicious."

"Of course I'm going to hurt her," Vicious said. Evil gleamed hotly from his eyes. "Deaf, huh? How do you know she's not faking it?"

"Dude, I've been watching her for some time now. They sign to her."

Vicious brought his gun up, and her heart jumped painfully, but she didn't move. This man was nothing more than a thug, and she was used to thugs. There were plenty in her grandfather's organization.

"No, don't kill her!" Cipher said.

"I'm not going to kill her. Yet."

Vicious placed the pistol right up next to her ear. Her heart hammered fearfully, but stayed still, already figuring out what he planned to do. She saw the thrill he got having her at his mercy. The fear excited him. He pulled the trigger. She didn't hear the blast but she felt the percussion of the weapon and a hot sting creased her cheek as the bullet exploded from the chamber. But she didn't flinch, and, slowly, he lowered his weapon.

She swallowed thickly.

Their eyes met, and the coldness radiating back at Kaiya left her chilled to the bone.

"Okay," Vicious said. "She *is* deaf."

"You're an ass," Cipher said.

Instantly, Vicious swung the gun up and aimed it at Cipher's head. The two men stared at each another for a long minute. Tension bracketed Cipher's mouth as he stared down the barrel of a loaded gun. There was not one doubt in her mind that out of the both of them, she'd rather it was Vicious who took a long walk off a short pier. He scared her. The craziness shining forth was dangerous and unpredictable — two deadly combinations.

She watched as Vicious suddenly began to laugh, and once again, he lowered his pistol. She felt slightly sorry for Cipher, who excelled mentally, but was vastly unmatched physically against the bigger, stronger man. A man like Vicious could never create a code as Cipher had done, never mind stealthily steal money from two separate entities.

Vicious glanced back at her, still chuckling. Up and down, he looked her over, lingering on her breasts, and bile churned in her belly. The last thing she wanted was his *admiration*. Kaiya folded her arms across her chest and lifted her chin.

"Ah, a little hellcat, I see," Vicious said.

She could practically feel the disdain oozing from his pours.

"I bet I could get bring out all her claws. Would you scar up my back, pretty girl, as I fucked your tight little pussy?"

She itched to slap the smirk right off his face, but she didn't want to reveal that she could read his lips. He raised his hand and brushed away a stray piece of hair off her cheek. Kaiya grabbed one of his fingers and bent it back, forcing his hand away from her. Revulsion rolled through her. His touch absolutely disgusted her.

Her defiance only seemed to excite him further. His whole body seemed to thrum with excitement. "Oh, yes, I'm going to enjoy taming you. And you know what's going to be even better? The look on Boone Tempest's face when he finds your used and broken body."

The next instant he had freed his hand and spun her around to level one arm against her throat and the other across her stomach. Kaiya used her nails to dig into his flesh, trying to get him to release her, but he seemed unaffected. Instead, the obvious pain must have aroused him even more because he ground his hard dick into her ass. She gasped, the arm around her throat cutting off normal airflow, causing her to thrust her elbow into his ribs. Other than a slight wince, he didn't move. It was as if he couldn't feel pain, and fear sliced through her. He wasn't letting her go and it quickly dawned on her that he was either going to rape her or kill her. She struggled, harder than before, desperate to tear away from him, but she just felt the rumble of his laughter, and her fear turned into full-blown terror. She was going to die, right here and now, without even getting a chance to tell Gabby and Boone how she truly felt about them. That she loved them. Completely, deeply, unending. Even after she died, she would love them, heart and soul. They'd taken a girl filled with suppressed rage and given her wings. They had set her free.

Pressure on her throat increased, and soon, she couldn't breathe at all. Kaiya clawed to escape, but he only tightened his grip. Her chest burned, tears flooded her eyes and she thrashed her body around in an effort to dislodge Vicious. It was the last desperate attempt at clinging to life, and she was failing. Her vision edged in darkness. Strength fled. Hope fled.

Then Cipher stepped up and placed a barrel against Vicious' forehead. Just as the world went black, the ricochet of gunfire bathed her again, only this time a warm spray of blood splattered over her. Hands fell away from her neck, and she drew in a deep, ragged gulp of air as she pitched forward into Cipher's arms. Kaiya coughed as she kept dragging in beautiful, precious air.

A few minutes passed before she got herself under control, and the fear of dying faded. She straightened and pulled away from Cipher. He still held the gun at his side. Kaiya looked behind her and saw the Vicious' dead body lying there, a large bleeding hole in his forehead, the skin around the mortal wound black from gunpowder. As she stared down into the lifeless eyes, she knew she should have felt something—shock, horror, disgust. But all she could summon was relief. She reared back with her leg and kicked the corpse as hard as possible, then she turned to Cipher and mouthed her thanks. Instead of smiling and answering, however, as she had expected, since he *did* just save her life, he raised his weapon and aimed it at her face.

"I know you can read my lips," he said. "Now that insane asshole is dead, let's go find my diamonds."

Diamonds?

Chapter Twenty-One

Cipher consulted the journal then held up a GPS locator, getting his bearings, before pulling her along behind him. He did this several times, navigating through the dense woods. Kaiya couldn't help but trip along the unmarked path as he led them farther away from civilization and a way back to find help. Not that she could ever bring the cops out here. Gabby and Boone were somewhere. She knew they had to be trailing them, and she'd never put them in a position where they could be arrested. No, the cops weren't an option, but what she wouldn't give to see her men come barreling toward them right then, although it was an unrealistic fantasy.

She'd been in this situation before, when she'd been kidnapped right outside of her hotel. Taken, without anyone knowing she was gone. It always made her wonder how a person could simply vanish without any trace of them left behind, but it had happened to her. She'd been a victim, and perhaps she'd always been one. First to a disease that took her hearing then to human traffickers. Then to her grandfather. But not this time. No, Kaiya knew if she was going to survive, she was would have to save herself.

"Here," Cipher said as they stopped by an old rotten tree. Cipher closed the journal with a snap. "I wrote the coordinates to this tree down so I wouldn't forget where I stashed this last bag because damn if all these trees don't look alike."

He tied the rope holding her hands together to a nearby branch then began to kick the dead tree over and over until the rotten wood splintered apart and tumbled to the ground. Another duffel bag spilled out. Cipher grinned and snatched it up gleefully. He walked over to her and squatted to open it. Kaiya spotted cash, guns and a several black velvet bags.

"Once I started filtering cash from the club and from the Master, I had to figure out a way to launder the money. So I invested in uncut diamonds." He held opened one bag and dumped a few ugly rocks into his palm. "Believe it or not, these are diamonds. Or you might call them blood diamonds. I call them a wise investment."

He laughed, and she was glad she couldn't hear how maniacal he must sound. Although she knew people invested in diamonds for a secure future, she doubted Cipher knew all the details of investing in diamonds, especially unpolished ones. Sure, they were a commodity that never really lost their value, but to get top dollar, he would need to know buyers, sellers and traders. Otherwise, a diamond engagement ring could be bought on the Internet for a fraction of its worth. Somehow, she really doubted Cipher knew the intricacies of the gem world, and she sure as heck wasn't going to bring up that line of debate. He carefully poured the diamonds back inside the bag, tied it then tossed next to the cash and weapons before standing to face her. He brought up his gun and leveled it at her forehead.

"I should shoot you. You've served your purpose."

Terror flooded her body. She didn't want to die, especially at *his* hands.

"But, those two shots had to travel and if I know Boone and Gabby, they're tracking us right now. If I kill you at this moment, they will hunt me down. I could wound you, but that gives me the same dilemma, and Gabby is one big asshole I don't want to tangle with." He lowered his gun. "So you're coming with me until I can get on my damn plane and get the hell out of here."

Plane? Where did he get a plane?

The questions tumbled around in her head as Cipher untied the rope from the branch, shouldered his duffel bag then yanked her to follow. They walked, and every once in a while he would consult his compass. Soon, the woods began to thin, and a moment later, they left the tree line behind and Kaiya realized they stood on a dirt runway. A large airplane hangar rested in the distance, with a single propeller, white plane staring at them. As he tugged on her roped hands to lead her toward the plane, a sense of disbelief washed over her. Did he pilot it himself? Did he plan on taking her with him?

A sign caught her attention. John Zinger Field. The letters from the lockers. Her mind raced on how she could possibly escape him. Out running him might be difficult, especially since her hands were bound with rope, but maybe she could hide long enough until he gave up and flew away in his plane. Maybe he was right and Gabby and Boone were tracking them at that moment, although she didn't want to put too much faith in being rescued. This very reason was why she'd taken self-defense, and she let the anger of being abducted simmer in her chest.

He dragged her forward and as they came closer to the airplane, Kaiya noticed a figure in a flight suit walking around the fuselage, checking on things. What surprised her immediately was the shock of blonde hair flowing down the pilot's back. Lisa was recognizable anywhere. Kaiya's mouth dropped open in surprise. Knowing she was the pilot just about made Hell freeze over, because if there were one person Kaiya would've said was a fluff piece of ass, it would've been Stone Cold's old lady. All the specific questions Lisa had asked now made sense.

As soon as Lisa saw Cipher, she let out a little squeal of excitement and ran toward him. Passionately, she threw herself into arms, planting little kisses over his face. Cipher had to drop the rope securing Kaiya to hold onto her.

"I can't wait to fly out of here, baby," Lisa said. "No more fucking old dick. Hello sandy beaches and Mai Tais!"

Cipher chuckled. "We're going to spend the rest of our lives living in swim suits, being waited on hand and foot."

"Oh, yes!" Lisa exclaimed as she gyrated her body against Cipher's.

Kaiya made a gagging noise.

The blonde pinned her with a fierce glare. "Right after we take care of business, that is."

Cipher took off the duffel bag and laid it at Lisa's feet. "It's all there. Almost every damn cent I managed to take from the Men of Hell and that fucking psycho, the Master."

Lisa knelt and zipped open the bag. In one hand, she pulled out a stack of hundred dollar bills and in the other, she held a baggie filled with uncut diamonds. "Beautiful," she murmured, her rapt expression reverently admiring her new commodity. "I've dreamed of this, you know. Ever since I was a little girl, I knew I was destined to be rich. I can finally live the high life."

"We can't go too crazy," Cipher said. "This has to last us."

Lisa looked at him and frowned. "We're rich, baby. We'll live like fucking royalty."

He shook his head. "Lisa, once we flee, Stone Cold will be searching for us. He has enough weight in the MC world where we'll have to lie low for a while. Until the heat dies down—"

"No!' she said, surging to her feet.

Kaiya followed their argument closely, waiting for a ripe moment to use for her own escape.

Lisa poked Cipher's chest. "The first thing we'll do is send Stone Cold a fucking Christmas card with a big, old 'fuck you'. Then we'll sell the diamonds and buy a fucking island! With slaves!"

Madness lined Lisa's face. Kaiya wondered if the crazy bitch actually realized how much money would be needed to own an island. And slaves? The woman was downright insane. Cipher jerked back and his expression quickly changed from lovesick besotted fool to unhappy calculating accountant. Yep, he was just learning his stolen fortune might not be so long lasting around his one, true love.

"You're not thinking clearly," he said.

Lisa slapped him across the face. "Don't use that tone of voice with me. I'm not crazy! I simply know what I deserve in life, and baby, I'm the best cocksucker you ever had on your dick. Remember how much you loved my lips wrapped around you?"

She went from insane girlfriend to simpering seductress in the blink of an eye. She trailed a finger down Cipher's chest and she pushed her breasts out a little, making sure her tits strained against the half-pulled-down zipper of her flight suit. He blinked, and Kaiya saw his IQ drop a hundred points when Lisa's mouth sucked on a section of his neck. Kaiya must have made a gagging noise because Cipher's eyes shot up and clashed with hers. Shaking his head slightly, he gripped Lisa's arm and dragged her away from where Kaiya stood, which was okay with her. No way did she want to see their PDA turn into outright fucking.

Left alone for a moment — or as alone as one could get in an open hangar — Kaiya knew she had to escape. If she didn't, she was dead, and she didn't plan on leaving her men behind, in this world or the next. She quickly worked on the rope binding her wrists, thankful for her small bones, until she managed to wiggle one wrist free from the rough hemp. The skin around her wrist was raw and bloody in some parts, but she ignored the slight pain as she quickly untied her other hand. Cipher and Lisa were talking by the plane, or arguing if the fierce expression on Lisa's face was anything to go by. The duffel bag lay only a foot away.

Carefully, Kaiya stretched out her leg and managed to dig her heel over the strap. Then she slowly, carefully, dragged the bag closer. Her heart thundered in her ears. When the duffel was close enough to reach, she rolled quickly, grabbed it and jumped to her feet, running as fast as she could.

She was sure they knew she was free. No way could they miss her taking off with their retirement plan. Kaiya reached inside the bag and pulled out the gun. Hooking the strap sideways around her body to keep her arms free, she quickly checked to make sure the gun was loaded and the chamber had a round in it. But how could she tell where Lisa and Cipher were if she couldn't hear them? She looked up. She needed high ground.

A storage loft was at the far end of the old hangar, and she made a running beeline for the stairs, keeping her back against the plane and equipment. If she could get upstairs, she could defend her position and hopefully take Lisa and Cipher out. Kaiya dragged in a deep breath to steady her hands. Well, she'd wanted to break out of the mold. Now she understood to be careful of what she wished for because killing two people might not be something she could ever recover from.

The silence overwhelmed her. When she'd first lost her hearing, the quiet almost drove her crazy. Now, knowing she was being hunted, but unable to figure out where the danger could strike, was a madness that almost caused her heart to explode. When the stairs loomed in front of her, she drew in a deep breath and ran for them, hoping that she wouldn't be shot down before reaching safety.

Almost there. Just a couple of feet. She was grabbed around the waist and spun around so fast that she slipped. A hand wrapped itself around her throat and squeezed, hard, cutting off her air. Her attacker hauled her to the side of the hangar where her back slammed into the unyielding metal walls. Another hand trapped hers holding the gun, rendering her helpless.

She looked into Cipher's pissed-off eyes and saw her death in their depths. All coherent thought fled. He squeezed harder, and her lungs burned with the need for oxygen. The edges of her vision began to darken.

Kaiya!

She blinked. Did she just *hear* her name? Or was it a moment of insanity forged from her dying brain? Who called out to her? Boone? Gabby? They were coming for her. She knew it, felt it in her soul. She couldn't let them find her body. She wanted to live, for them. For herself. For the future they could create together. She brought up her knee and hit Cipher hard between his legs. His whoosh of breath fanned across her face, and he loosed his hold on her as he slumped over to cradle his dick and balls. It wasn't much but it was enough to wrestle the gun free, and she wasted no time pressing the barrel against his forehead and pulling the trigger.

The reverberation of the gun echoed through her body. Blood splattered across her face and chest. But not one ounce of remorse hit her as she watched Cipher fall dead at her feet. She dragged in a great lungful of air, coughed a little since she'd almost been strangled *twice*, then ran. She didn't know where Lisa was, but she knew the woman was close. Just as she made it out of the hangar, someone tackled her to the ground and when she landed, the gun slid out of her grasp.

Kaiya didn't have time to mourn it as she was flipped over. She stared into Lisa's hate-filled blue eyes.

"You bitch!" she raged. "That was my man! He was taking me away from all this club bullshit! He was going to keep me in diamonds forever."

She couldn't even tell Lisa that she still had the diamonds and that she could pilot the plane, that she didn't need Cipher at all. The woman punched her, and Kaiya's cheek exploded in pain. For a moment, she swam in and out of consciousness, until Lisa grabbed a fist full of hair. The sharp pain roused Kaiya. She stared wide-eyed into Lisa's eyes. For a moment, she was transported back to that night where Boone had fingered her and the gazing connection with Lisa had pushed her into climax. That sensual moment was now gone, and all Kaiya could see was evil and hatred. Lisa rested the barrel of a gun against her forehead.

"You're dead," she said.

Kaiya couldn't look away. She screamed, unable to bottle up her fear.

Then Lisa's eyes widened, and she jerked forward. The gun fell harmlessly. And Lisa's dead body draped over her like a heavy blanket.

Kaiya pushed against the woman, unable to find traction, until Lisa was pulled away to lay dead beside her. Kaiya blinked and looked up first to see Eagle then Stone Cold, who reached down to help her stand. Only her knees wouldn't hold her and they buckled. Eagle caught her and helped her away from the scene, away from Lisa's dead body, where Kaiya sat heavily on the runway.

She stared at both men, unable to comprehend at first that she was still alive. But had these men saved her only to kill her now? Her body shook and her heart pounded. She felt like she was going to pass out or vomit. Maybe both.

"We aren't going to hurt you, Kaiya," Eagle said. She blinked and watched his mouth as he repeated what he said.

She glanced at Stone Cold, who squatted next to Lisa's body. Blood soaked the ground around the woman, mainly around the head. Eagle touched her shoulder and she looked back at him.

"I knew Lisa was having an affair with Cipher," he said. She read his lips. "I told Stone Cold. He was going to confront her when the three of you showed up and he wanted to see what you knew about that man. The whole joining forces was, at first, a ruse to get information out of you. But I think he really warmed up to the idea."

Kaiya flicked a quick glance at the plane. She couldn't help but wonder how they'd known about this airfield.

"The plane belongs to Stone Cold," he said.

She raised an eyebrow at how he could read her mind.

He grinned. "I'm very good at reading people. That's how Lisa was brought into the club. Stone Cold recruited her from piloting school. He wanted someone to run his product by air."

He brushed the hair away from her temple and once again, unease slithered down her spine. However, he let her pull away and gave her a rueful grin.

"I'm glad we got here in time," he told her. "You're a beautiful woman, and I can see you're loyal to your man."

She didn't even try to correct him. He might have eagle eyes on most things, but he didn't see everything. Eagle looked over her head and nodded.

"I see your man and bodyguard are here just in time to save the day."

Kaiya whipped her head around. Boone and Gabby ran toward them. She jumped to her feet and hurried to meet them. Happiness swelled in her heart and each beat pounded their names. When she finally met them, they swept her up in a tight embrace and her arms went around both of their necks. They almost crushed her with their fierce hug, but she didn't care. She was back in their arms and that was all that mattered.

A long moment later, they finally pulled back. Boone kissed her hard on the mouth, then it was Gabby's turn. It almost broke her heart when she felt the trembling in his lips.

"Are you all right?" Boone signed.

She nodded and began explaining everything. When she pointed behind her, both men looked up and their whole demeanors changed as they spotted Eagle and Stone Cold. Gabby actually moved in front of her, protecting her with his body. She placed her hand on his arm and his muscles were granite, hard and unyielding. Still, she never felt as protected or as loved in that moment.

Boone led the way to the two Whiskey Knights men. Along the way, he pulled his gun free and held it loose at his side. From what Kaiya had told them, they'd saved her life, but it still didn't diminish the fact that because of them it had been threatened in the first place.

He took in the whole scene in an instant. Lisa lay in a bloody heap on the ground. Cipher's body not too far away. Stone Cold glared at his gun.

"You lied to me," Boone said. "Every facet of your hospitality was a goddamn fucking lie!"

"I just saved your woman's life!"

"Just tell me why the fuck I've been running around in the woods when you apparently knew to come right here."

Stone Cold shook his head regretfully. "Listen, I wanted to tell you, but I needed information first."

Boone brought the barrel of his gun up, aiming directly at the man. "Not helping."

Stone Cold threw up his hands. "All right! Cipher came to me after you cut off his tat and exiled him. By this time, Vicious decided to prove he had the balls to rise in rank and had left. I knew he was going after the Men of Hell."

"You told him to come after my club?" Boone demanded.

"I never told him to take over another club."

"But you never told him not too," Boone surmised.

"That kid had ambition to rise in the Knight's ranks, but he was too crazy to ever be considered." Stone Cold shook his head. "The fucker burned up one of the prospects because he stepped on his boots, for piss sake! No one was going to turn over the reins to him."

"So you cut him loose."

"Yes," he said. "At the same time, Eagle found Cipher at the bus depot. Brought him to our compound to heal and, I admit, I wanted information about your club."

Boone took in a deep breath, fighting against the rage that wanted him to pull the trigger and be damned with the consequences. "And after Vicious and Bizerk tore apart my club, you still didn't come forward. How convenient that Vicious and Cipher became the best of friends."

"I swear I had no knowledge of that. Not until today."

"When your old lady decides to fly away with her much younger lover and millions of dollars in stolen money."

The other man flicked a gaze at the dead woman. Her blonde hair lay matted in streaks of red. "I knew about her and Cipher, but I figured why not let her have some fun. It's not like I haven't had my cock sucked by other women."

"But she threatened your club."

"Still," he said sadly. "I loved her."

"Then you know how pissed I am about Vicious."

"Yeah, Boone, I know I've not been very forthcoming with you, but—"

"But nothing," Boone said and forced himself to lower his gun. "You did save Kaiya's life, and for that, I won't kill you. But no deal can exist between the Knights and the Men of Hell. You need to use the interstate, I suggest you get past Bair as quickly as possible."

Stone Cold nodded, as if he had expected that. "What about Cipher's loot?"

"What about it? Cipher stole the money from the club, as well as from the Master. It belongs to the M.O.H."

Stone Cold gave a crooked grin. "And yet you're on the Knights territory."

Boone hauled his fist back and let it fly, the blow landing squarely on Stone Cold's jaw. The older man fell back.

"Don't fucking push it," Boone said coldly. "Good-fucking-bye."

He turned and marched away. Gabby took hold of Kaiya's hand and the three of them left the clearing. After a few minutes, Boone stopped and sighed. He ran a hand down his face.

"Fucking hell!" he shouted. He glanced between her and Gabby. "I have no fucking idea where we are and the last thing I want to do is go crawling back for help."

Kaiya grinned and reached inside the duffel bag. She pulled out the GPS system and held it out to him. Boone took one look at it and hugged her. What had he ever done to deserve such a smart, beautiful, fierce woman?

Well, he wasn't going to question it too closely. He had no desire to look a gift horse in the mouth.

Epilogue

"I can't understand him," Gabby said.

Kaiya smiled at him. "Because he's signing in Japanese."

She turned back to Red Eye. They'd arrived the day before and almost immediately, she recognized the fact that the old man was deaf, although he probably wouldn't be able to talk even if he could hear. The teeth left in his mouth were all black, his hands shook like crazy, and he had a habit of staring off into space. But he was smiling and grasping imaginary butterflies, so at least he was happy in his high.

"Classic sign of testing his own product," she signed to Gabby and Boone.

Boone nodded and turned his head to hide his amusement. She actually felt sorry for Red Eye. The man probably had been a brilliant chemist once upon a time. Red Eye jolted back to reality and greeted her again, which he'd already done once before.

"You are very pretty," he signed clumsily then lapsed back into his happy place.

"He likes you," Red Eye's wife said. She was dressed in traditional Japanese couture, wearing a *yukata, obi* with *tabi* socks and *geta* shoes. It was amusing to see Gabby and Boone trying to fit around the traditional tea ceremony. The old woman had taken one look at Kaiya and had brought out the *matcha* powder to perform *chakai*, which was good since that was the more informal of the tea ceremony. Otherwise, her men would have to endure several tedious hours with Red Eye and his wife, who happened to be a shrewd negotiator.

"Will he be all right?" Kaiya asked with her hands.

"Oh, yes. He does not produce traditional meth," his wife signed. "He's found something a little different. New. It is a good medicine."

The drug was anything but medicinal, but Kaiya kept her thoughts to herself. "Has it been tested?"

"Oh, yes," the wife replied, signing quickly. "He always tests on himself first before selling his batches."

Kaiya eyed her husband. "Quality control?"

The wife graciously bowed. "If he dies, it was a bad batch."

Kaiya had nothing to say to that and shared a quick glance with Gabby and Boone. Kaiya had heard that Red Eye made something different, and so far, he seemed to be very happy with his new version of the drug. His recipe was something new, something different, but looked to be just as potent, and Kaiya recognized the profit margin to be had. Amidst the whole tea drinking, Kaiya managed to strike a decent deal for their product.

When they left later that day, Kaiya bowed to Red Eye and his wife as if they'd concluded an informal gathering. The three of them sped away, and Kaiya let her mind wander as she watched the countryside pass by. The raw diamonds were tucked safely in Gabby's saddlebags and she had plans on how to get them cut first before selling them. All her research suggested that they would sell better if they were market ready, so she had some research to do on finding a gem cutter too. The business of selling diamonds wasn't one she was familiar with, but she did know the acquisition of the raw diamonds would set the club up nicely for years to come.

They crossed the US-Canadian border before pulling over for the night. The hotel wasn't one owned by the Men of Hell, but it was nice enough. Once they got their room, Boone and Gabby dumped their saddlebags on the floor. Kaiya stared in bemusement at them, knowing that they contained probably a few million dollars in ugly, uncut stone.

"Interesting couple," Boone signed.

Kaiya nodded, pulling her thoughts back to the meeting they'd just had. "She is the business brains while he is the cook."

"You have no problem with how the Men of Hell make money?" Gabby asked.

"No," she signed. "I grew up at my grandfather's elbow. I have sat in on many similar negotiations. Plus a few a little more...cutthroat."

They ate that night in a small steakhouse next to their hotel. After they'd filled their bellies with good food and lots of beer, Gabby and Boone each took hold of one of her hands to lead her back to their room. The last thing she had wanted to do was spend the night in Sioux City, or Omaha for that matter, so they planned their trip back along the scenic route, using the single lane back roads. It might be a longer trip, but this way Kaiya knew they would avoid any other complications.

She was done with adventure for the time being. All she wanted now was to cuddle up to her men.

Once inside the room, Boone locked the door behind them, shutting out the world. They had all showered earlier when they'd come off the road, and now sweet anticipation flooded through Kaiya. Her nipples hardened with desire. Her pussy juices ran. She bit her lip, waiting for her men to claim her.

Gabby captured her exploring hands and laid one of them on his heart. He cupped her face and brushed his thumb over her lower lip, then he bent his head. Their mouths met, a soft merging at first, but the fire that always existed between them flared. Gabby rested his other hand on her hip to bring her snugly into his body as their kisses grew more passionate. Behind her, Boone touched her and she gasped at having both men surround her. Their relationship may have started out as a way to break free of the mold she'd been forced into, to prove to herself that she wasn't a good little girl anymore, but her emotions had morphed into more than desire, more than simple lust. She craved them both, needed them as much as she needed oxygen to survive.

She unbuttoned Gabby's jeans and eased down the tab so she could reach inside to find his long, stiff cock. She released him from the unyielding denim. Behind her, Boone kissed her neck and divested her of clothing. She wiggled her hips to get her pants down and her panties slid with them to land in a puddle at her feet. He bent and helped her out of them, tossing the material aside. Then he opened her legs wider and parted her ass cheeks.

The next instant, he swiped his tongue over her rosette, and she let out a gasp of pleasure. Lust shot through her. She might not have worn the butt plug, but it didn't seem to matter because Boone was all about stretching her. He left for a moment, and Gabby used that opportunity to take off her shirt and bra. She stood before them naked while they were still fully dressed. Boone returned and resumed his position, and this time a dollop of cold lube plopped into her crack. He smeared it over her anus before pressing inward. She squirmed, just as Gabby bent to take one nipple in his mouth. She lost her grip on his cock, so she buried her hand in his hair, pressing him close. After a few minutes, more lube dribbled on and he added another finger to stretcher out even more. The burn rushed through her, so she tried her best to relax.

Gabby moved back to undress, then he sat on the edge of the bed and beckoned her with a finger. Boone withdrew his fingers and slapped her on the ass, which made her jump. He guided her forward until she was close enough, then he pushed her head down to Gabby's cock, which stood at attention. She happily complied, holding the base to slide her mouth over the head. Slowly, she engulfed the huge dick, moving down the shaft, going as far as she could go. As she withdrew, she pumped her hand up and down as she lavished the mushroom head, sucking until her cheeks hollowed.

A moment later, Boone ran his fingers through her pussy lips to find her clit. He rubbed the bundle of nerves until her juices ran and she moaned around the big cock in her mouth. Then Boone placed his dick at her pussy entrance and pushed forward. Taking hold of her hips, he fucked her. Fast, hard, deep, in and out of her slick passage, filling her until her orgasm rushed toward the surface. He reached around her to pinch one of her nipples, and her climax exploded through her, bringing a hot flush over her skin. Boone withdrew from her body. He hadn't come yet, so she wondered what he was doing, but figured it out as Gabby pulled her from his delicious cock, toward him. His dick stood straight up, slicked with her saliva, waiting and seeping with pre-cum. He guided her to straddle him, and her already sensitive cunt quivered as his hardness slid through her lips, bumping her clit, to slide home. For a long moment, they sat there, face to face, staring at each another until Boone pressed against her back.

Gabby lay back, reaching up to play with her nipples. There was a short pause, then she felt more lube around her anus. Again, Boone eased his fingers inside her and Kaiya's breath caught at the feeling of being stuffed full in both holes. Soon, she knew it would be his cock. She had dreamed about this, had fantasized about it night after night. The wonder of it was even more fulfilling knowing she was with two men who cared for her and whom she was fast falling in love with.

She saw a condom wrapper flutter to the ground and she looked over her shoulder to see him slathering lube on his wrapped dick. He stroked himself a couple of times, winked at her then pulled her ass cheeks apart. Her heart hammered and her breath came in short little gasps of excitement. The tip of his penis touched her sphincter and instinct had her wanting to pull away. But she took a deep breath and pushed back, relaxing, and her rosette gave way and opened enough for the head to slip inside. His invasion burned slightly, but he held still, letting her adjust.

Gabby said something, because she felt his words rumble through him, and figured he was talking with Boone on how to proceed. He eased her back off his cock, which allowed Boone more space to penetrate deeper. Then he slid out, and Gabby slid in, until she caught hold of how they planned on double tapping her. As one went in, the other pulled out, back and forth, like a well-oiled machine. Kaiya could barely comprehend the incredible sensations rolling through her, as both men possessed her. She'd never felt anything even remotely resembling the feelings generated by these two men. Boone leaned over her back, kissing her neck, while Gabby nipped her swollen clit between the fork of two fingers and very gently stroked the tip with his thumb.

They had started out slowly, taking their time as she adjusted to the double penetration, but little by little they increased their speeds, quicker and more forcefully until she was jolted forward each time by Boone's thrusts. Having two cocks inside her, knowing they were only separated by a thin membrane, stirred her excitement and lust to a whole new level. Sweat rolled off their bodies, and they fell out of sync with each other as each man now chased his own plateau of pleasure.

Boone plunged harder and faster in her rectum just as Gabby stiffened and swelled inside her. He came with a shout she couldn't hear, but she could feel the vibration through his body. Hot streams of cum flooded into her vagina until it overflowed. Then Boone buried himself in her ass and she felt him groan as he came. The double sensation was too much for her. Her own orgasm swept over her. Wave after powerful wave of bliss poured through her until she sagged onto Gabby's still-heaving chest.

Boone withdrew from her and she watched as he took off the condom and headed for the bathroom. Moments later, he returned with a wet washcloth, helped her off Gabby and fell to his knees before her to clean up the cum running down her thighs. It was a very intimate gesture that had her heart bursting with love.

She lay panting in the aftermath of fantastic sex, sweat drying on her skin.

Gabby picked up her hand and laced their fingers together. "When we get back to Bair, I'm going to put in a request to the V.A. for a therapist."

She squeezed his hand, indicting she'd read his lips and understood his words.

"I didn't want to admit how weak I was," he continued. "I thought I could handle everything on my own. That maybe, somehow, I deserved the madness for being such a coward."

"You are not a coward and you're never alone," she signed. "I will *always* be with you. And what you're dealing with doesn't make you weak, Gabby. It turns your bones to steal while your heart heals."

He gave her a faint smile. "I love you, Kaiya."

"I love you too, Gordon Dixon," she said aloud.

Boone rolled to his side so he that he loomed over her. "Don't forget about me. I love you too."

"Never, my love," she signed. Then she took a deep breath and said, aloud, "It is the three of us."

"You've got the most beautiful voice I've ever heard," Boone murmured. He placed his hand on top of their intertwined ones and smiled.

About the Author

I like writing about the very ordinary girl thrust into extraordinary circumstances, so my heroines will probably never be lawyers, doctors or corporate high rollers. I try to write characters who aren't cookie cutters and push myself to write complicated situations that I have no idea how to resolve, forcing me to think outside the box. I love writing characters who are real, complex and full of flaws, heroes and heroines who find redemption through love.

I've been pretty fortunate in life to experience some amazing things. I've lived in France, traveled throughout Europe, Australia and New Zealand. I am a mom to an amazing little boy. I'm surrounded by friends and family. And although I love holding a book in my hand, I absolutely adore my e-reader, which I've named Ruby. I love to hear from readers so I've made it really easy to find me on the web.

Beth D. Carter loves to hear from readers. You can find her contact information, website and author biography at http://www.totallybound.com.

Home of Erotic Romance